PRAISE FOR ~~SEASON OF THE~~ MONSTER

"READER BE WARNED, GOOSEBUMPS INCOMING."

"The mystery is thick in the air while the thrills keep you guessing and the horror chills you. Truly spine chillingly eerie. AJ Humphreys has done a great job with Season of the Monster - hopefully season(S)."

— LIZ JOHNSON | AUTHOR OF *TENEBROUS*

"FANTASTIC STORY"

"The imagery is so vivid you are RIGHT there!"

— RACHEL ROY | AUTHOR OF *PARALLEL WORLDS*

"EXCELLENT READ!"

"I really enjoyed the atmosphere that the author makes. It has a true spine-tingle quality that seems all too rare these days."

— AMAZON REVIEWER

SEASON OF THE MONSTER

PART I | SPRING

AJ HUMPHREYS

Season of The Monster | SPRING was originally produced serially through Amazon's Kindle Vella platform.

Amazon Kindle Vella Edition / February - May 2022

First Print Edition / ISBN 979-8-9867050-0-2 / August 2022

Cover Design: AJ Humphreys

Cover Images: Canva Pro Stock Photos

❋ Created with Vellum

For Everyone Who Has A Little Monster In Them.

Keep Fighting.

CONTENTS

PART I | SPRING

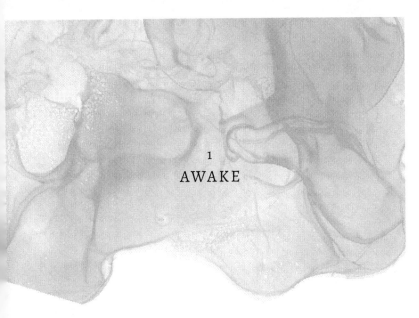

1

AWAKE

R iding the bus has been an easy adjustment for Ghini despite the brutal winter. Still, she is grateful to finally have Spring here. Being able to trade in her puffy coat for a loose-fitting cable knit sweater that highlights how much weight she'd lost is genuinely satisfying.

She has hardly sat still these past six months, missing more meals than she ate. She knows that most people will attribute the weight loss to depression, which she prefers to the truth.

Sure, she's depressed, but she's had to soldier on, and the real reason behind her lack of appetite stems more from her Adderall addiction and constant sleep deprivation than anything else. It was the kind of involuntary weight-loss plan, where behind closed doors, she laughed at herself with icy notes of self-deprecation.

As the city bus traverses the Deadwood Yellow Route, the sky has gone the familiar grey color that Rapid City always produces this time of year. It'd probably rain over the Black Hills tonight, but if she was lucky, she'd be able to get back on the bus before that happened. Though, in the grand scheme of it all, she knows there are worse things than a little water.

If anyone knows that, it's Ghini Freeman.

When she's dropped off at the factory, she must prepare herself. Her standard ritual is to stand outside the giant monolith inhaling and exhaling several deep breaths. She does this to steel herself for the barrage of *Red* that the Coca-Cola High Country Bottling Company uses to assault its workers.

Inside the employee breakroom, which doubles as a locker room for personal effects, are plastered the words "Honor God In All We Do." Those faded red letters feel like the most egregious slap in the face. Because Ghini had found God, she *had*.

After being a reality-TV cast-off, she spent a long time indulging her newfound wealth on several vices in the hopes of easing the sting of being dismissed from the hit show, *The Real*. She moved back home to South Dakota and enjoyed life as a local celebrity. Well, celebrity was whitewashing. She was a sex symbol for the modest nightlife community to take advantage of, which she had been more than content with.

Then she'd grown wider as a wannabe rapper gave her the greatest gift of her life. Her little girl, her gift from God, whose picture stares back at Ghini each time she opens her locker. In her sight, Ghini dawns her red apron and hairnet. The loose netting feels silly considering she has given up on doing anything with her hair, preferring it buzzed short and neat.

"Hey there Ghini? How goes things today?"

Oh, Todd. She can't help but laugh inside. She knows he has a thing for her, but she doesn't have time for luxuries like that. Yet she appreciates the man. He's cute the way a pug is cute. She thinks of him as her little work puppy. Friendly, loyal, and a bit annoying at times but overall she does love him for all his kindness. Albeit a platonic love. Still, she is glad to have him in her life.

"Hey Todd, how're the boys doing?" Todd coaches the local AAU 14-Under Basketball Team. Todd had been a Division 1 College athlete himself, but that was only due to his size. Standing close to seven-feet tall, he had been meant for basketball. But he was perennially overweight and had the bad knees to show for it. So after a long battle with the bottle, all he had left to himself now was coaching.

"Great! Took home second at the Custer Court Chaos this past weekend! Thirty-two teams from the Dakotas, Wyoming, and even two from Nebraska. I tell you what that was one stanky gym though. Too small a facility for a couple hundred thirteen-fourteen-year-old young men. Unfortunately, those Bismarck boys were just a bit too much for our boys. Plus Devon rolled his ankle in the semis, it was the second half thankfully. We were down size after that point. If it'd been in the first half, couldn't even been sure that we'd've made it to the finals. But we had the lead late enough that Tae could come in and hold off the big men. Sure proud of those boys though, wish ya could've seen 'em."

It's always nice for Ghini to be distracted by Todd's anecdotes. She knows most of the boys, after all, Devon especially. The boy wasn't just tall, he was a genius. He was going to be the main reason that her baby girl made it to High School in the fall. He'd been the best tutor she could find. But now they'd all be moving on without her little Jeannie —

"How'd you spend the weekend? Same as always?" He asks, his big pug eyes bulging above the somber note in his voice.

"Same as always." She says feeling that somberness reflected in her own voice.

"Any new leads?"

"Thought so." Not that she believed it. "Someone called in

seeing a young black woman in the Hills, looking tattered and lost, but the description didn't match. Too old."

"Sorry Ghini. I'm sure something will turn up. Faith tells me the Lord'll protect her. Just gotta be patient. I'm certain of that. On the drive, I even listened to this Podcast about some Smart girl in Utah that was held captive for like a year or something, but she was brought home safe and sound, so I'm sure there's still, ya know, hope for Jeannie. The Lord, He does work in mysterious ways."

She feels more disheartened thinking about her baby girl being kidnapped and kept alive to be tortured all as part of the Lord's plan. If all this is truly what the Lord had in store for her baby girl, it was hard to have faith in Him.

WHEN SHE AWOKE LAST WEEK, she had felt like one of those baby horses from those nature videos. The ones who walk funny cause they don't understand how their lanky legs work. She now knows it's been over six months since the woman with the leopard spot eyes. That's the last thing she remembers before the long dreams began.

There had been the dark place, where she met the royal queen. The queen who scarred her and kissed her. She'd yet to ever kiss a boy, but the queen's intoxicating kiss lingers all the same. She feels confused. She has never looked at a girl before and felt anything like how she felt looking at the boys in her class. Yet, since waking, she often finds herself tracing a slender finger across her lips, longing for the queen's once more.

She recalls visions of men wrapping her in a coffin like the mummies at the museum. A see-through prison where she watched the queen leave, while her men stayed behind to protect the tomb. She was finally coming to accept that none of this was a dream, even if it still feels like one. She can hardly bring herself to accept that this is her body. She looks like her mother does on those old VHS tapes that she's not supposed to watch.

Save for the eyes.

Those, she isn't sure she'll ever feel comfortable seeing in a reflection. Thankfully, sunglasses were easy to obtain. She knows those eyes are with her forever now. Just like these new hips, her pronounced breasts, and slim waist. Though the latter traits are a bit easier to grow accustomed to.

Meanwhile, there is still that one thing she has yet to bring herself to do. She wishes there was another route she could explore, but it feels as if she's exhausted all other options. The hunger pangs are only getting worse. Nothing tastes good either. She'd picked fruits and vomited. She'd tried plants only to suffer the same result. She'd stolen snacks from a gas station, but only the sugary candies held a palatable taste. But it never satiated her.

She knows what she has to do. Walter had given her the instructions with his last breath. Just before curling up into a pile with the other *drones*, or so he'd called them. But the hunger was ravaging her insides, and she feels it may finally be time. There's no point in avoiding it any further. She'll start with Walter. He'll be the most fresh, being the only one who'd survived through the winter.

She knows instinctually that she has a job to do, and she needs her strength to do it. Time is limited after all, so if she wants to live, she has to accept that it is not only her right but her responsibility to be the queen.

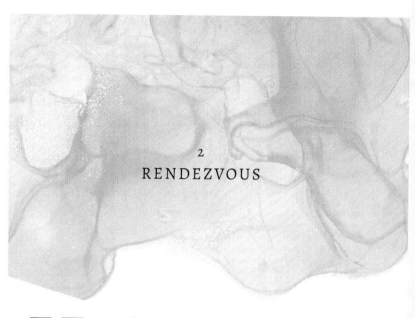

2
RENDEZVOUS

His watch reads 11:47. It's always like clockwork, these little rendezvous of theirs.

Sure enough, the bus turns the corner. Its bright fluorescent beams slice through the subtle fog of the evening. But he doesn't wait for her at the stop anymore. It's not about being a gentleman and impressing these days. It's simply ritual. Not romance.

At least this time, Detective Dak Johnson has real news to share.

She joins him on the bench, which has a fine layer of dew accumulating on it already. Neither of them minds though he feels guilty for not having wiped it down. His mother's voice echoes disapprovingly somewhere beyond his reach.

He takes out a cigarette, and she, one of those cheap replaceable gas station vaporizers. Except it doesn't work. It died on her during the evening's shift. She's forgotten the charging cable too, much like she's forgotten the little device has already run out of charge.

"Didn't have the right cable at work," Ghini says shaking

the black plastic. He knows this is an ask, and he slides out another stick. She leans over his lap, blocking the evening chill, as he obliges her silent request for a light.

She smells of vanilla and syrup. "Thanks." She adds with an exhalation of smoke into the cool night air.

They sit in silence, staring at the bleak gray and clay brick-work of the Rapid City Public Safety Building. They used to sit out front, but Detective Johnson had needed to get away from the building.

So, they sit across the road now. Always the same bench on the lawn of the State Historical Society. The lawn is bigger here, and there are more trees. It's quaint, though, somewhat of a safety nightmare for the officers across the street, but there's never been an issue.

"Grab the wrong cable again?" He says awkwardly fracturing the silence. She nods. It's still not exactly comfortable between them. "Damn cables. I got a different one for everything. You'd think these kids out West would design one universal doo-hickey."

She chuckles. His humor is dry, but she likes dry.

He knows she doesn't enjoy the cigarette though. He knows she'll spend five minutes washing her hands to get the smell out. But this was their ritual. Nicotine first. Brass tax second.

She's got enough of a buzz and stomps out the remaining third of her stick.

He looks to her and begrudgingly puts out his, placing it behind his ear, pinched in place thanks to his thick pulled-back dreads. They both know he'll relight this last quarter before going back inside.

"Listen Ghini, I hate that we went on a goose chase this weekend. But, the lead was solid. Then this morning, I get this call from a Uni."

He pulls the large smartphone from inside his coat. The damn thing's too large. Johnson wishes the department would just issue flip phones again. But that era is long gone. "There's something that you need to see here."

She's nervous as he opens the photo gallery. Ghini doesn't know what to expect, but after six months she has yet to learn how to tamp down optimistic expectations.

The photo is a grainy still from inside a gas station, but the subject is perfectly framed, looking up at the camera, not trying to hide. The hairs jolt up the back of her neck, as she realizes what she's looking at.

Herself.

Well, a younger self. But it's herself. She's lived in the past enough to know that much.

"Dak. That's —"

"Impossible?" He adds when she can't seem to find the word.

"Yeah. Impossible."

"My thoughts exactly. Look, I know this is crazy, but listen, that's you." Johnson pauses, wary of choosing his next words carefully. "Sorry, let me rephrase that. That," he says poking a fat dry finger at the screen, "is the spitting image of you. A doppelgänger."

"A doppelgainer." She struggles with the word, though she's too confused to care. "That never had no kid. That didn't ruin her life by being aksed to do no reality TV." She can hear it. She's working herself up.

He sees it. "Listen Ghini." He's not looking at her but through the well-lit road to the station. "I'm just putting the facts before ya, as a courtesy." He sets the hefty phone on her thigh. "But this is the same day as the tip we got. Fits the description too. Did you look at her clothes?"

She brings herself to the phone. It's hard to make out

because the angle of the black and white still is from a ceiling camera, but her fingers stretch the image further. The woman's clothes look stained and blotchy. They're tattered and stretched tightly over the woman's curvy figure.

Ghini can't help but envy.

Then she notices it.

The *doppel-whatever* isn't wearing a crop top and capris like she'd thought. They're pajamas. Not just any pajamas.

Jeannie's.

They're stretched to fit the woman's form but Ghini recognizes those stripes anywhere. If it were a color photo, she'd bet her life that those stripes would be green and gold.

She sees the woman wearing them, but she can only picture her little girl.

"What's going on?" The tremble in her voice too apparent to them both.

"I don't know. I'm an old dog Ghini. Been doing this a long time, and seen a lotta things that I'd never want nobody to see. But this. This hurts my head. Cuz my gut." He pauses. The final commitment to what he'll say next. "See, it's hollering that that's Jeannie. But how's she go and grow up a decade in six months?"

She's lost for words. This is something out of a Netflix show. This can't be her life. She stares into the face a bit longer, and then a shiver reverberates from her core.

"What's wrong with her eyes?"

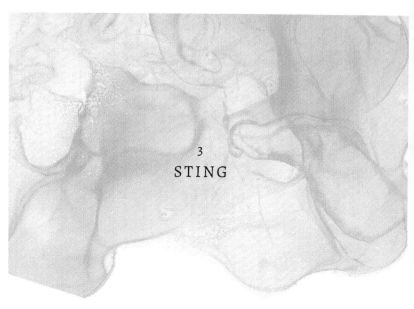

3

STING

S he's revitalized with the first rays of the rising sun. Her body knows when to wake her, and exhausts itself into the deepest of sleeps whenever nightfall hits.

She feels uncannily strong this morning having finally eaten and dressed. Thankfully, Walter had tried to be thorough. There is an entire chamber with clothing of different sizes. He had thought of most everything.

For all of it, she is grateful. She wishes they'd had a bit more time.

It would have made last night harder.

The first bite had disgusted her.

But the second. It ravished her. She felt something she'd never felt before. It was similar to the queen's kiss, except rather than incapacitating her, it drove her. One was a euphoric laziness, the other a passionate adrenaline.

She'd bitten down with a growing tenacity each time. The joints pulled apart with intoxicating ease. She fed on it like a turkey leg at the county fair. When she was done, all that was left were bones and scraps. She'd made a mess of herself but she was satisfied and had finally slept without hunger pains.

Despite waking early and refreshed, she regrets how long she spent cleaning herself up in the stream. But now she looks presentable. That's most important. She looks forward to eating this evening. She hopes it's as pleasurable of an experience as the night before. She also needs company. She needs to begin the —

What'd he call it?

He'd broken it down.

Ass. She giggles to herself.

Mill. She nods.

Tion.

Ass...Mill...Tion...Assmilltion...Assimilation!

Unfortunately, she hasn't seen a single soul on the trails this morning. Maybe she missed them. The world does look different now. Fuzzy. Low definition, like a VHS tape. But the colors, they're more . . .

More what?

She can't quite describe it. Rather than blending, colors appear distinct. The subtle difference in greens and yellows and blacks and grey seem to distinctly pop.

"Hurry up Kari!" A man's voice echoes against the valley stream where she sits. It's a funny voice. It sounds like a Disney Prince to her ear.

"Why don't you just wait!" A lady's voice responds, soft and irritable. "For God sakes woman." The man's voice grows louder but sounds so proper to her ear. "This is a seven miler, we can't just mull about."

The lady groans. It's quiet, but she hears it.

She hears a lot of things.

Her eyes may have gotten worse, but her hearing seems so much better.

"Jason, we're not even enjoying the hike. It's not about mileage, it's about the journey." Kari sighs again. A reverberation that glides down to the stream and settles in her chest. She feels sorry for this Kari. "At least let me take some photos."

"Fine." He, Jason, speaks as if this is a chore. The way she'd have spoken if her grandmother said she had to clean her room for guests that would never even see her room.

Then she spots them. Their colors are vibrant in contrast to the world around them. Blues, oranges, and unnatural greens and yellows.

The two hikers are further away than she first thought. Her depth perception is only good up close now. They're nothing more than colorful blurs floating beyond the tree line.

"Jay. I think someone's out there."

How close are you?

"Hi, there!" She hears herself say. It's the first time she's spoken in what feels like an eternity. She's still not used to the deeper, stronger voice she'd inherited from her grandmother. "Just out enjoying a beautiful spring morning?"

The man is tall, but then the lady is too. She can't make out their features, but when she waves to them she can tell that the lady waves back.

"Hi there, ma'am."

Ma'am . . .

The woman's face comes into focus as they near. It's all high definition now that she has something to focus on. She's so young. Both of them are. Probably students on break. They're both white, but her face is gentle with soft lines and freckles. The boy's though, his is harsh. A strong jaw line, acne scarring, a patchwork of stubble, and a permanent frown make him seem unapproachable.

"I'm Kari." She pronounces it like, *Car-ee.* He'd said, *Care-ee.* "This is Jason."

He doesn't say anything. Instead, he's fidgety. He doesn't want to be here. He feels uncomfortable. She can strangely feel it. A sensation under her skin.

There's silence. They are waiting on her to introduce herself, she realizes.

"Come on Care-ee." He says it with disdain before beginning to walk off.

But she doesn't let Kari do the same. Her hand grabs the girl's with a speed that surprises even herself. It's instinct. Kari lets out a little whine, as she squeezes.

"Just call me Queenie." She says.

There's a burning chemical sensation in her fingertips, boiling, aching for release. A release that comes as Queenie drives her nails into the girl's hand. Kari whimpers once more. Jason doesn't even look back.

The girl nods with a smile etched in fear, trying to pull away. But Queenie can't let go. She needs to do one last thing. She slowly pushes the stolen sunglasses down the bridge of her nose, exposing her eyes. She watches with joy as Kari's pupils swell against the colorful threads of her iris.

"Your eyes. They're. They're. They—" She trails off.

Queenie whispers. *"Tomorrow morning. Meet me in this same spot. Tell no one."*

Without a word, she releases the girl, who turns and totters off the way she came.

"Care! Where are you—*what the*—"

"Don't mind her. Worry about yourself."

Queenie is on him before he can even register her movements. But it's her strength that seems most inconceivable as she lifts him high into the air.

Her fingers are warm inside his throat as the last pulses of his Adam's apple fade against her palm.

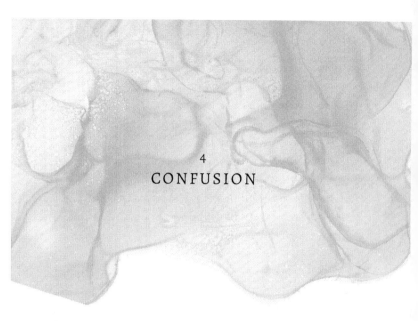

4

CONFUSION

T hat morning, when Kari looked over to the stool she'd been using as a nightstand since her days in pigtails, she was unnerved with how early it was.

Normally, she'd be lucky to wake when her alarm goes off. But this morning, she'd somehow risen without it. Maybe for the first time in her life, she's up at the crack of dawn without any help to stir her.

She still doesn't remember going to bed. It's as if she'd been in a fog. There's a faint recollection of bickering with Jason, then bupkis until she woke.

Yet, here she is. Driving Jason's Outback to — to — she's genuinely unsure. Thankfully, the GPS isn't. So, without a worry, the car seems to navigate itself to the back of an unfamiliar parking lot. All that's here are an abandoned trailhead and its forlorn campsite.

Her feet carry her across the rocky pathway leading to the heart of the hills. On autopilot, innate directions seem to guide her like how a turtle just knows where to go to spawn each year. Or how their young know to find the sea upon hatching.

The deeper she gets, the more she begins to feel a sense of familiarity nagging at the back of her neck. As if the primitive little brain back there directs her instinctually.

Something's off.

The world seems blurry. How is she only now noticing? Have her eyes been like this all morning? If she focuses on things near her, she can make out their details, otherwise, it's all a blurry patchwork of vibrant colors.

Maybe I need an eye doctor?

The thought fades. She hears buzzing, and the fluttering of wings. The spring breeze rustles fall's weathered remnants across the forest floor. There's another sound in the distance.

Water.

She *needs* to get to that water. She's a bloodhound on the scent. The trail melts away as her feet fly her through the tree line. She leaves the rocks and ascending pines for the open expanse of valley and stream.

A figure in the distance moves and Kari's eyes focus. A young attractive black woman sits atop a log crossing the stream. Her sunglasses shield half her face, and her huge smile, displaying pristine white teeth, takes up the other half. She waves, encouraging Kari to continue forward.

Queenie. My Queenie.

She feels as if she's returned home for the holidays, the sense of joy and familiarity is confusing but welcome.

"Well, hello hello beautiful." Queenie's voice comforts her.

Kari struggles to find the words. Her mind is still foggy. All she can muster is a sheepish, "Hi." She feels like she did that time she met the Jonas Brothers when she was twelve. She's drunk off her own emotions.

Queenie hops down, almost floating the distance to reach

her. Like a loving parent, she embraces Kari, holding her head the way only a mother can.

She smells good.

It reminds her of her grandmother's snickerdoodles.

"You must have so many questions."

Kari does. Except she's not sure what they should be.

As she lets go, it's apparent that Queenie's waiting for her. She watches Kari with infant-like wonder in her eyes.

"Um. I don't know."

"Duh!" Queenie's palm echoes off her forehead. "I'm sorry! I'm new to this too, and it's really complicated, ya know? Plus, I didn't know what to expect, but thankfully you look the same. I think. Which is good, I guess. Like I think that means I chose right. But, I don't have all the details down just yet. There's just so much to remember."

Kari finds this strange gibberish endearing. Like the ramblings of a little girl.

"I have to kiss you now, okay? And then we'll do the last part."

Without warning, Queenie's warm lips envelop her own. It's better than sex. At least better than sex with Jason. Though, it probably wouldn't matter if she'd been bedded by Idris Elba, she can't imagine anything reaching her core with such intoxicating passion

When Queenie breaks away, Kari wants more, though she knows she can't have it.

"Wow."

"I know! It's the best kiss you'll ever have. Guaranteed!" She giggles. "But you're not going to change like I did. At least you're not supposed to since you're already a woman."

Kari wants to be confused, but things seem clear, even her sight seems more detailed. That's when memories begin to return. She was *here* yesterday.

She'd left alone. She'd driven home. She'd gone straight to bed. She'd ignored her grandmother. Though she recalls the old woman's joy at not seeing Jason.

The morning floods in next. A score of thoughts and emotions that seem foreign almost alien to her send her mind spinning. Physically, she's beginning to feel light-headed and is worried that she might faint there on the spot.

Where is Jason?

She focuses on Queenie. The memories ease away like a receding tide. Just looking at Queenie alleviates her stress. Tranquility ebbs into its place and calms her. Kari feels a need to please her. If asked, Kari would jump without hesitation down to the exact millimeter requested.

"Okay Kari, now's the hard part. But you'll adjust to the taste really quickly. It's actually super yummy."

She knows my name. And she said it right.

Her infatuation grows. She never wants to lose this feeling, and she'll do whatever it takes to protect it. To protect *her*.

My Mother. My Queenie.

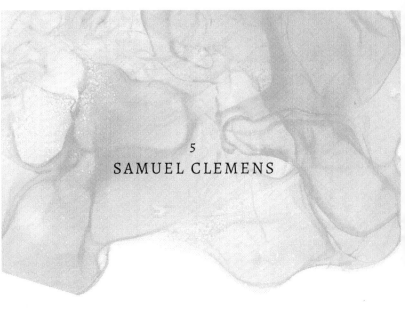

5

SAMUEL CLEMENS

When Ghini gets off work, she takes the Deadwood line to its final stop and walks the remaining quarter mile to *The Watering Hole*. A podunk bar on the edge of the bustling old cowboy town of Deadwood.

The town's changed a lot over the years, modernizing, and assimilating to the tourist era. All except *The Watering Hole*. The *lone* exception. Embracing rustic western decor, the place is right out of an old John Wayne flick.

Normally, drinking her sorrows away on a work night was something best left to the couch, a bottle of Cabernet, and a large fleece blanket. But tonight she needed something that only *The W-H* could provide.

Samuel Clemens.

The old man sports the same mop of white bushy hair as the famous author but lacks the voluptuous mustache. His weathered and worn face comprises a latticework of wrinkles. The deep lines show through patches of clean stubble that border on fuzz.

Though he looks older than he is, he *is* as wise as he looks. Samuel Clemens was that person who knew everything in the hills. Despite being the bar's majority owner, he tended the bar nightly, finding enjoyment in being the sounding board for the buzzing of barflies.

During the day, he works in construction and landscaping. Despite a true love for working with his hands, supervisors often ask him to don other hats. Having Samuel there to shake hands and ask for signatures was always an asset. With a poker player's ideal face, he was often an ace in the hole for negotiations and complaints.

Floating around so many circles, it was a wonder how often people would talk carelessly around *Old Sam Clemens*. So, he heard it all. He knew all the happenings and everyone's stories. With that, his greatest asset was a picture-perfect memory. If he heard it or saw it, it's likely he'd never forget it.

This is how he'd known about Ghini long before Ghini knew Samuel. As a bartender, and a man amongst men, Ghini's story had made its way through the grapevine years before Jeannie's disappearance.

Knowing what he did, he'd been kind to her throughout the ordeal. On more than one occasion he'd even driven her to search parties after she sold her car. He'd also pulled strings to help her get the job at the cola plant.

Despite feeling indebted to him, this wasn't a selfless visit. If anyone would know what to do next, it'd be Samuel. The old man is the only person inside the bar when Ghini arrives. As always, the bar reeks of stale alcohol and cigarettes. Smells forever soaked into that dark wood that the bar had originally been built with.

Behind the bar, Samuel's washing glasses with the only clean linen the bar probably owns — a paper towel.

She pulls up one of the heavy oak stools. "I'll take a glass of the Buffalo."

"Two fingers?"

She holds up three. He nods, and their quiet transaction moves forward.

While he has his back to her, she slips an Adderall into her mouth knowing that she probably won't sleep again tonight, but she needs her wits for this conversation.

Samuel slides her the drink. "Four buck."

The friends and family discount.

She pays with a twenty, insisting he keeps the change. Money may be tight, but Ghini knows karma goes around.

The smooth spicy sweetness of the whiskey forces out an audible sigh as the amphetamine slides down her throat.

"Well?" Samuel's not much for sentences.

"Something's happened, Samuel. And." She searches her vocabulary. He's as patient as ever. After another sip, she gives up, "I can't explain it. So, I just have to show ya."

She pulls out her phone and stares at a picture of herself from a different life. It's a version that only brings back painful memories. But Samuel needs to see it to understand what she's talking about.

"So, this is me. Fifteen years ago or so, but it's me 'ight?" His stoic face doesn't betray a single thought. Not even that he has seen this photo many times, thanks to drunken patrons and blowhard concrete pourers.

She slides over to the next photo from the surveillance footage. "This was taken at a convenience store over the weekend."

He doesn't say a word but leans forward. Curiosity shows on his white bushy eyebrows. "Well, I'll be."

He swipes back and forth on the two photos. "Thought this'd be bout those missin' hikers." He swipes a few more times. "But this certainly's more intrestin'. Ch's'why a man should never assume." He slides the phone back.

This is the first she is hearing of missing hikers, but they're not her problem. Hikers always go missing in The Hills. They either turn up or they don't.

"So?"

"You wanna know if I think that's Jeannie?"

She feels the flush of embarrassment replace the flush of the whiskey. It's warmer and stings with painful memories. She prefers the whiskey. She empties her glass, *a double gagger*, as her old man would have called it.

"No, I'm not aksin'. It *is* her. It's my *likkle girl.* I just need to know *how."*

Samuel glides the bar's length and pulls a long slender bottle from a cabinet beneath.

"Eagle Rare. Aged 17 years."

He grabs two glasses and pops the cork, pouring three fingers for each of them.

"Has to be enjoyed in a fresh glass." He knocks her glass with his own and sips the rich amber mixture. It's got the rugged scent of a man. Like it was brewed in a leather barrel with cigars.

"I do."

She's not sure what he means as she chases the firewater with a sip of air.

"I do think it's her." At this, they both take another sip. In the silence, she takes a second to revel in the thought that maybe she isn't going crazy. "I do. These hills're special." He looks out beyond her. The lights of the town shine enough for an outline of the hills to form on the horizon.

"Ya came to the right man Miss Ghini. I'm not the one to tell ya what ya need." A quick sip. "But I know the one that is."

He finishes the drink in one final gulp.

"A waste."

Without another word, Samuel begins tidying around the bar, leaving Ghini unattended and confused.

Just when she's about ready to ask for more, he looks at her with pale eyes and says, "Go home. Line's almost done for the night. Get some sleep, and meet here round noon. 'N call in sick ta work, ya won't be goin' in tomorrow."

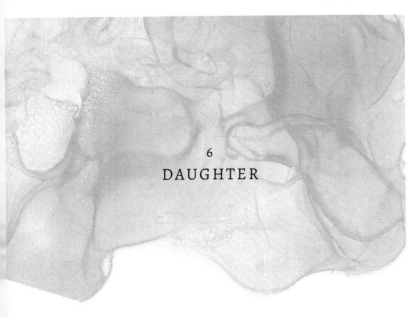

6

DAUGHTER

The crackle of dried mud splitting snaps Queenie from her reveries. She catches the thin muddy chrysalis fracture with the eruption of gorgeous slender fingers.

A nagging voice reminds her how strange this all is.

The entirety of the fragile tomb begins to crack like a strike of lightning. Shortly thereafter a chorus of thundering debris echoes off the cave's walls. All she can do is watch with joy as her firstborn bares herself to the world.

Kari had been a cute girl before — girl might be a stretch — driver's license said she was twenty-one. But now she's the spitting image of radiance and womanhood. Queenie wishes she had a better word to describe how she felt about her newborn's pristine figure. Unfortunately, her mind only gravitated toward the one—*obsessed.*

Her hips have widened beneath her newly shrunken waistline, which accentuates the change. Kari stands there, shivering, in nothing but her underwear. Any trace of fat seems to have melted off her bones, most significantly her face, which now reveals a strong square jaw. Queenie thinks of those old Tomb Raider movies, except Kari's hair is sandy and her lips are smaller. Among other things.

Then there are her eyes. She isn't sure Kari even realizes it, with each blink they flip. They swell into an elongated alien blanket of hazel, honeycombed in oblong black pupils. Then as if nothing had changed, a single blink shrinks the colorful tapestry, restoring the whites to her eyes, with only a single oily black orb at the center of a hazel ring.

The change fascinates Queenie. She feels a strange instinct guide her over to her newborn daughter of a woman.

Is this what being moms is like?

A part of her wishes her mother was here with her in this moment. Queenie thinks she'd be proud of her, though she knows it's not possible. So, the next best thing is for her to embrace the desire to be there for her own baby girl. Yet, there's Walter's voice inside her head, uttering reminders of how it needs to be the other way around.

"How do you feel?" She tenderly clutches her daughter's head to her chest. Body-to-body contact infests her with a desire for more. More family, more bodies, more of *this*.

A soft purr answers the question for her, still, Kari clarifies, "Amazing."

It's true. She's never felt so incredible. Not even the lingering thoughts of their — *meal* — the night before can trouble her. She can almost feel the pleasure of it all again.

"Come! Watch the sunrise with me!"

Queenie grabs her daughter by the hand, pulling the girl from their cave like a sled dog. At its mouth, they catch the night's lingering purple glow as it caresses the scene of hills and prairie.

The morning light nourishes them both. Queenie stretches to the sun, thinking of beansprouts in a cup.

Kari knows it's the Vitamin D that vitalizes them both. At least that's the rationale forcing her mind to move on.

"Queenie?"

"Yes, my Kari." But before her daughter can reply. "Oh my! I forgot you don't have clothes. Poor girl." She runs back into the cave, returning as quickly as she'd disappeared, carrying an arm full of clothes.

As Kari dresses, Queenie leaves the cave and dances from stone to stone, buzzing her way down a rocky path. She hops and spins down to a seat on one of the many large boulders littering the area. There, she waits as Kari, finally dressed, trots along like a curious puppy.

"Queenie . . ."

"Yes." She says with a smile large enough to share.

"What are we?"

"That's a toughie, honestly." Queenie taps at her chin. "We're whatever we want to be! We're um, what's the word. I know it — TER-SHE-AIRY! That's it we're tertiary consumers. Ya know the ones that fill the tiny triangle at the top of the food pyramid."

Kari chuckles. She's reminded of middle school diagrams. Food webs — or *was it chains?* And the cell diagrams. There were so many diagrams back then. Irrespective of these reveries, part of her urges, almost violently, to get her answer.

Conflictingly, she doesn't want to upset Queenie either. She understands her answer to a degree. Her body *has* blossomed into a powerhouse overnight. *Apex predators* is the word coming to mind.

The world seems clear, both visually and mentally for the first time in her adult life. She has purpose. It's a purpose that Kari hadn't known since Scooter. She'd have done anything for that little pug, but she'd do *more* for Queenie.

"Okay. But what picture would kids use for us — would it

be — ya know?" She mimes a hiss with her incisors, simultaneously holding her hands up like claws. Her fingers look the part. They seem longer, more slender. Then she notices her nails. They look *sharper*.

Queenie laughs. "Yeah, I don't get *that*, but whatever you're thinking's likely wrong." She hops down from her stone and begins twisting and twirling her way down the trail. Her hair bounces and bobs like a gentle black cloud.

"So, if we're not, ya know." Kari tries to keep up. Though, she still can't bring herself to say the word because it seems too ridiculous. "Which I guess makes sense considering we're just walking around in the sunshine — what are we?"

There's a pang of frustration for Queenie in having to deal with the questions.

This must also be what moms feels like.

She wants to play in her world. She finally has a friend to share it with, there's no reason to spoil it now.

Though Walter was very clear, *choose your first wisely.* She thought of school days. Thoughts of Devon Pettway and Linett Jenkins. *Those* kids. Who would always sit at the front and ask *all* the questions. If Kari was like that, then Queenie was sure she chose right.

Unfortunately, Queenie couldn't bear to give up any answers. Not yet at least.

"We're — a *family*. A *special* family." She says, sliding Kari's slim and tender hand in her own. With willing ease, Queenie pulls Kari in close, so she can see what Queenie sees.

There, on the edge of the trail, atop tenuous footing, they peer into the valley below. "We've been given a gift. A gift that makes us strong. A gift that makes us family. But we have to grow our *likkle* family." She laughs to herself.

"Okay." There is a part of Kari that needs more. That little know-it-all who craves answers. Except that part of her doesn't seem so strong anymore. More like it's drowning. Fortunately, making way for the part of her that wants to focus on Queenie.

"Listen. I know that's not, like, the best answer. But, I hardly know what's going on, more than basics. Which, I guess, you prob'ly want me sharing." A toothy grin highlights high cheekbones. "So. Anywho. Rule one. No leaving after sundown. The dark's harder to see in now, trust me. Anyway, I need you close — *always*." Kari's hand molds itself to Queenie's dark slender fingers, as her mother grips tighter. But she needs the girl's gaze. She pulls Kari's attention to her own eyes and watches as they flutter from honeycombs to a singular pit.

With maternal pride, Queenie experiences the beat of Kari's heart rate through her own fingertips. But the sound, the rapid *thuh-dumps*, is the experience she struggles to label.

Maybe, *intoxicating*. Though she has no experience with such a feeling.

"Rule two. We do *not* go out in the cold. The cold is like alcohol for adults. It makes bad decisions and can cause the sleepies."

"The sleepies?"

"Yeah. Ya know. When like you can't keep your eyes open and stuff. Like when you're doing this." She mimes dipping her head and jolting upright to stay awake.

That Kari understands. She'd seen Jason do it plenty. Laughing, Kari adds, "*the sleepies*." She feels such affection for her Queenie. She wants more from her. She'll give anything to get it.

A chorus of laughter spikes in the distance and both women spin on their heels like a synchronized figure skating routine. Kari is aware of her eyes pulsing now. To her, the sensation is subtle, but the effect is drastic. With minimal concentration, she feels these orbital cameras in her head focusing simultaneously. Apertures open and close at high speeds, letting light flood in and out. With ease, she dials down to a perfect zoom and focus to notice movement in the distance.

"Last rule for now." Queenie draws Kari's attention back to her. "No boys. Not yet at least." Kari giggles. Once again reminded of school days. But Queenie is serious. Kari can feel her mother's stare bore into her. "As I was saying. No boys. But girls are okay. If you meet good girls for the family, just like, let all that light into your big hazel eyes, and stare into theirs. They'll *do* —" She pauses, not liking her word choice. "*Understand* whatever you need them to. Think of it like hypnosis."

"Easy enough." Something isn't sitting right with her about this, but focusing on it is impossible with Queenie needing her.

"Bet. One more thing. If a boy gives you a hard time. They — *understand* easier. So, bring him home for dinner."

Queenie's fingers extend and flex displaying the long, barbed nails of her right hand. They almost seem to *pulse* — like a fluid beat beneath the surface.

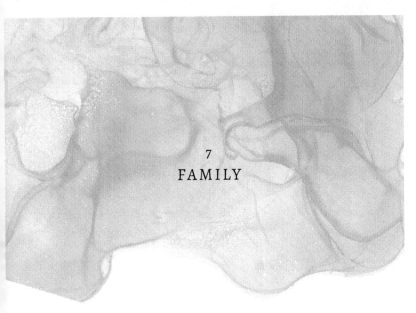

7

FAMILY

"You know it's crazy that I never been out here before."

The mounds of ancient Earth — textured by water that no longer remained — slide past them as they wind their way further and further into Badlands National Park. The striations of the rock mix rustic reds and purples with beiges, browns, and yellows. Sights entirely foreign to Ghini.

She wonders if this is where they shot movies of alien worlds.

"You know this is abouts where they found Sue," are the first words Samuel utters in nearly an hour.

She's not sure who Sue is but feels embarrassed not to know.

Maybe another missing girl.

Though, she has doubts that's correct. So, Ghini takes a page from Samuel and keeps her mouth shut. They've mostly sat in silence for two hours anyway, so what difference would it make?

With Samuel behind the wheel of his old gray F250, Ghini

has sat listening to the radio, scrolling through social media. Though she can hardly stomach another second of squinting at the screen.

The road's twists and turns seem endless until the terrain finally gives way to a level valley.

A heard of big horn rams sit next to the road close enough that Ghini has to halt the impulsive itch to reach through the window toward their elegant horns. A bit further down, two males earn their namesake. The sounds of thick collisions echo along the prairie as they strike one another with ferocity.

"Dominance."

"What?"

"The males. They do it for dominance. Prove who's the alpha."

"Guess it don't matter animal or people, men always fighting each other."

Samuel cracks a smile, which is as good as a hearty laugh coming from him.

Up ahead a lone buffalo saunters down the center of the road, while a flurry of prairie dogs waggle their way from one side of the pavement to the next. Samuel slows the big truck until forced to halt, letting the parade of round fluffy butts scoot on through, before skirting around the hairy behemoth.

The leather creaks slowly in his hands. Easing passed, Ghini's close enough to see the beauty of the giant's features. Its thick duotone hair matted into wooly knots, while an untamed goatee reminds her of Jeannie's father. She thinks how they even have the same hair — a big poofy afro. It looks better on the buffalo.

As they pass, she notes the gentle eyes. Giant brown globes, uninterested in the old rustling truck easing passed.

Jeannie would love this place.

It's not long before they're entering the heart of nowhere.

Known to the locals as Interior, the place is a tiny ghost town. Every road, dirt or gravel. Some both. A perpetual wake of dust seems to cling to the air, thus coating the town. There's an ominous sense of abandonment.

There are a few trailers here and there, a couple of old farmhouses, and by the looks of it, two churches. Maybe a bar as well. There are plenty of cars and two old Winnebagos parked out front of what she suspects must be the local's watering hole.

"Who are we meeting here Samuel?"

His frenzied white hair shifts with the car, while his tanned deep leather wrinkles fail to betray any emotion beneath. "We're going to be visiting a relative a mine."

She had never thought of Samuel having family. To her, it was as if the man had just appeared one day — fully grown and wisened for the pleasure of the old cowboy town of Deadwood.

"I didn't know you had any family out here."

"Never asked," he says calmly.

A pang of guilt flutters under her chest. "So, who is this family?"

Failing to give a response, Samuel pulls the truck to a stop outside the more shambley looking of the two churches. It's the epitome of a textbook's stock photo for old one-room church houses. A white coat of paint fails to hide rotting lumber. Missing panes of glass have been haphazardly replaced with duct tape and beer boxes.

"That's for them to say." He kills the engine and with deliberate strength, hops down from the cab.

Ghini slips an instant release under her tongue and tries to follow, but the seatbelt whips her back in place, nearly causing her to choke on the Adderall. Fingers fumbling, she struggles to get the old and fraying restraint from its holster before clambering down.

Samuel hasn't waited either. He's already at the worn double doors, hitting Ghini with another wave of embarrassed guilt. Awkwardly, she speeds passed a statuesque Samuel standing just inside.

There, she feels the uncomfortable itch of dust caking her rich skin. Stopping to scratch, she takes in the house of worship. It feels bigger than it looks, and up on the dais is a young effeminate-looking boy in work pants and a cutoff flannel shirt. He's building something.

Only when they're right on top of him can she see it's a meticulously handcrafted picture frame. "Did you carve that?" She hears herself ask.

The boy doesn't look up, but his voice is as feminine as his face. "Yes ma'am. Painted 'at 'un too." He points to a picture of Jesus that looks like prints she'd seen at a Wally World.

The carvings are so detailed and intricate. Crosses and wreaths, and other holy items — whose names now escape her — intertwine to form a beautiful wooden mosaic.

"Wow. You're amazing. I gotta ask you to make one for me." The boy stops and looks first at her then Samuel. "I'd pay you, course." She throws in nervously.

"Sam." He nods, "who's *this?*"

"Samuel'll be fine Bernice." Ghini feels a puzzled look stretch across her brow.

"*Bernie. Please* don't get petty on me Uncle."

"Apologies. Bernie."

Bernie knows well enough to address the elephant in the room. Which, in their mind, should be this stranger that has bombarded their day without so much as an introduction.

"Bernice is a dead name. Please, just call me Bernie. And *only* Bernie."

"Oh yeah, no worries homeboy." Inside, she cringes, thinking that was probably too much.

One of her makeup gals on *The Real* had been trans, and she was a great woman. Always so helpful, so kind. Ghini *adored* her. *Annette.* She always had the best wine, best gossip, and best nails. Oh, how Ghini missed her long nails sometimes, but this is not the time.

This moment is more important to her. She needs to know why she just sat in a car for two hours without so much as an explanation. So, Ghini makes the mental note: *he, him, he-him, hehim.* She knows Samuel didn't drive out here to discuss gender studies, but she's not sure what this boy has to do with Jeannie.

"Bernie this is Ghini. Ghini, Bernie."

"Like Lamborghini?"

"Exactly." Her mother's favorite car.

"Cool." There's a wry smile on his face.

Two Clemens smiles in one day, the world must be ending.

"'Nuff introductions. We need your help. Ghini's daughter, *thirteen*, mind, 's'caught up in that same mess." He says sitting down into the first row of pews.

The boy's eyes grow wide, and he gestures for Ghini to follow his uncle's lead. Like the hip professor she'd known at Rapid City Community College, Bernie plops himself down on the dais' edge.

With his face back to the family's trademark vacant stare, Bernie mutters, "I'll answer questions. But just know, if the colony has her—at that age—there's nothing left to be done." He takes a bite out of his fingernail. The whole white bit peels away, before soaring off his tongue when he adds, "Sorry for the candor. But, ya know, truth sets ya free 'n all that." He nibbles at the nail again. "If I was you, I'd just plan the funeral and move. Far. Far as possible."

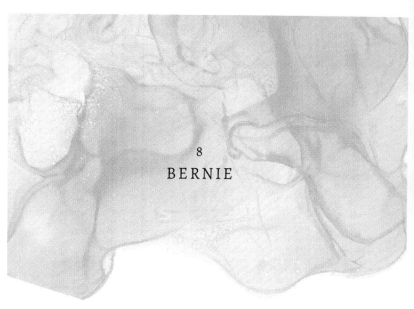

8

BERNIE

"When I was little, my mom was everything a kid could ask for. She made her living working all the tourist traps. She was a staple, my mom. She did Crazy Horse, Rushmore, Custer, wherever she could. She loved it out in the hills. I did too.

"I never had a dad, so she took me to work most days. I got more n' more freedom as I grew. First, it was, *stay in the break room*. Then, *feel free to explore round the grounds*. Fine'ly, *just be back by five*, or somethin' like that.

"So, one day. I'm twelve, maybe 'leven. Probly twelve. It's a be back by five sorta day. She's at Crazy Horse, working the tacky gift shop. So, I go for a hike.

"Now, most that land you're not s'posed to hike, cuz they're constantly demoing the rock. But I was an adventurous little brat. So I sneak off. Had my stupid little plastic Crazy Horse watch keeping me on schedule.

"I go exploring the groves of trees and stone that Mr. Horse looks into. I got a real good internal compass. Plus, y'know, I was an over-confident little shit, like I said. So, I ain't worried bout gettin' lost or nothin'.

"That's when outta nowhere there's this lady. Now, I know *I'm* not s'posed to be there, but she's more outta place. She got pretty name-brand clothes and bundled up like it's the middle of winter, even though it was start-uh fall.

"She just sits there. *Staring*. She got on those big Goose n' Maverick sunglasses even though it's cloudy. Then she waves. Like she knows me or somethin'."

There's this look consuming Bernie's face as he speaks. Ghini knows the look. It's the, *what if I'd done something different* look. He's fidgeting with his thumbs, worming side-to-side on the edge of the dais. Though Ghini hasn't known him more than a few minutes, she knows in her gut that this isn't normal behavior.

Bernie's eyes shift to his uncle as if to say, *do I have to?*

Samuel heaves a sigh, pulling a flask from inside his thick denim coat. With a quick gulp for himself, Samuel passes the dented little container off. Ghini knows she's not the world's best parent, but she can't help thinking Bernie's a bit young.

Gulping down a sidecar of air, Bernie tries to hand the flask back to his uncle. Instead, Samuel motions with a nod of his head, signaling for Ghini to take it next. She gives it a whiff.

And — it — is — *strong*.

It reeks of pure alcohol. She can't stop flexing her cheeks, as the lingering scent singes her nose hairs. She relents to a swig and immediately regrets it.

She hands Samuel back his flask, which he takes a casual pull from, nonplussed while she still struggles with the after-burn.

"Thanks, Unc. So —" Bernie takes another pallet-cleansing breath. "This woman. She, uh — She starts asking me all these questions. Weird 'uns. How old 'm'I? Why'm'I alone? But then's the one that sends shivers up my back. I wasn't a dumb kid, ya know? Reckless sure, but not dumb. I'm cautious of her but hadn't been too worried until she asks, *'have ya had your first bleed?'*

"She says it just like that, lingering on each word. And. Well, it weren't unusual for a girl at that age, I don't think. 'Cept that's what she *wanted* to hear."

Ghini shivers, her concern mounting. The vulgarity of it infuriates her. She'd expect some disgusting man to be that obtuse, but not a woman. Okay, girls maybe, but Women? Never. The scene in her mind spreads a scorching rage along the underside of her skin.

In her anger, her thoughts drift to Jeannie who hadn't started her cycle before she —.

Women were catty. But, little preteen girls could be *cruel*.

Her poor Jeannie had it especially rough. Lagging in the transition to womanhood, the other girls had found it funny to call her a baby, leave diapers in her locker, hang pacifiers on her backpack — someone had even glued a babydoll to her desk.

Thankfully, Jeannie had inherited some sort of resilience from deep within the gene pool. She'd come to Ghini with her plan, and together they stocked her backpack with all the monthly needs. Jeannie would tell her how she went so far as to accidentally drop a stray pad or flash a jingle of *Midol* once or twice a month.

Except now . . . now it sounded like Jeannie was the perfect target for this — *kidnapper*.

"I should have never answered that question." He's paused once more, the quiver of his eyes betraying his vivid reverie. "She's fast, this woman. She's on top of me as soon as I answer her. And I mean on top of me. I'm lying on the ground before I

can register it. My head's swimmin' from the hit. Then I'm
brought back with this searing, *toxic* pain in my arm.

"Her fingers are in my shoulder. *Here.*" He pulls up the
remnant of his sleeve. Visible on a pale shoulder is an arch of
four large crescent scars. A fifth, fatter one, violently ridges
out near his clavicle. "They're *in* there, up to the *nail bed.* I
tried to fight. Swear I did. Tore my arm up good too.

"Then she does the thing. Haunts mosta my dreams." He
trails off. There's a lifeless gaze glossing over his eyes as they
drift to the ceiling. Ghini has no clue what the boy's thinking
about, but etched into his face, is fear.

With silence consuming the room, Ghini notices the sun's
glare shimmering on thin wisps of peach fuzz peppering
Bernie's face. She takes him in a bit more. He's got a farmer's
tan that says he's never been outside without a shirt on. His
eyebrows are overgrown and bushy. He's got a wrestler's nose
— thick, bent, and busted. With a case of cauliflower ear to
match. There are other scars too. She's embarrassed with
herself for prying into the boy's past with her gaze.

Though she's well aware he's not a child anymore, the
mother in her can't help but yearn to care for him.

Why's he out here all alone? Where was his mother? Were
all of these scars from this one woman? And if this is what she
could see, *then what couldn't she?*

He's still looking to the rafters when the silence breaks.
"Her fuckin' eyes." A fragile silence permeates the air for a
brief second. "Know how if you look at someone's eye just
right you see the pupil is just like a hole, and the colored part
is all these noodles or threads or ripples or whatever? Yeah,
well her eye was like a honeycomb of that. Not a drop of
white. The noodles wormed their way through her entire
eye. So, it was full of these brownish-amber threads. And
instead of one pit, she's got this collection of oval-ey stop-

sign holes throughout. I don't even know how to explain it right.

"But thems the last thing I remember. Next thing I know, I come to in this cave. Her eyes, then cave." The snap of Bernie's fingers echoes off the rafters above.

"My body aches like it's been through a mix of tetanus boosters and manual labor. There's no hope of moving. Pain's doing its thing if I do so much as move my eyes. So I sit there, leaning against the surprisingly warm wall of rock.

"For hours, I stew in this muggy cave, like it's middl'a August swampy hot. Then I notice there ain't no other kids here. Plenty of grown women, and three times as many men. They're living here. Shit's everywhere: clothes, furniture, blankets, candy wrappers — lots of pop cans and candy wrappers.

"Anyhow, I try screaming, but it's painful. Don't matter though. The men don't look at me. Seem like they can't even hear me. It ain't avoiding, the men don't notice a single thing I do.

"That's when the other woman shows up, and she's — *frightenin'*. Her body's all warped in ways that don't make sense. She's pale, showing all that God had given her. Though she don't look natural. I can see her ribs, but she looks strong. Her thin arms look like they're filled with steel cables. Her legs, same shit. Her abs are stones stacked in a caved belly under those bulging ribs.

"She's built like a cartoon. Her waist was about this big around." Bernie connects pointer fingers and thumbs to make a circle no bigger than a large candle. "I thought it had to be bad plastic surgery like on tv. But I know it weren't."

Unfortunately, Ghini knew exactly the type of work Bernie was talking about. She'd once thought to have it done herself.

"Her face was skeletal. What's the word? *Gaunt*, I think. Her jaw's uncomfortable to look at. It's just hard. She's got no padding. Her head's kinda shaped like home plate on a baseball diamond. But her eyes. They're those same honeycomb eyes, 'cept hers are green.

"I remember wanting to cry but couldn't. Everything, emotions too, were just frozen. She grabs my chin with long slender fingers, forcing her stare on me. Don't think I could've looked away from 'em if I'd tried. The whole world disappeared into those black pits.

"Then she kisses me. It's a kiss that tastes like good whiskey. It's intoxicating and it burns but in that good way. Spicy, and sweet. There's this flutter in my stomach. I want more. A hunger for more. So bad I ached. Images flash across my mind — bite my lip, pull my hair, instinctual shit. Animalistic shit. I 'member those feelings clear as day."

Ghini notices Bernie rubbing a finger across his lips. She doesn't think he even realizes. "She's mad when she pulls away. No that don't do it justice. She's damn furious. She starts screaming. Callin' me a liar. Then she grabs the woman who brought me there by her hair and drags her across the floor. Strangest part? The lady don't fight it.

"*I'm sorry my queen.*' She says in this boring voice. Then this Queen-or-whatever, rips the woman from the ground, danglin' her in the air like a little fish before thrusting her hand *through* the other woman's chest. Easy as if she were made've drywall. The dying woman's eyes drain back to normal and the color leaks outta her. Then the naked one tosses her aside like a sack of junk. I remember, her body thudded twice.

"Crimson dripping from the alien curves of her body, the naked lady just wanders off. I see her say something to a group of men, but she don't wait around to see what happens next."

The air stretches with tension that seems to split open when Bernie says, "They pulled her limp and ragged body apart like a cheese stick. When they was done, I ain't see nothing but scraps of flesh and bone left."

Bernie takes Ghini's gaze now.

She *knows* he is an adult, but she can still see the remnants of a child in Bernie's dull green eyes. She gets up to hug him, but Samuel grabs her wrist. His calluses scratch at her dry skin. He shakes his head once and nods for her to sit.

"Thanks. But I just. I don't like touching people. Or them touching me. Doctors been hard enough." He looks down toward the floor. "Probly see why."

Ghini nods and allows the foreboding silence to creep back in as she retakes her seat.

"So, how did you escape?" She eventually asks.

"Just walked out in the middle of the night. Think they forgot about me. Never saw the Queen-lady again. Think I know why though. I didn't notice till I finally got outta the woods and to a washroom."

He pauses and lets loose a whisper, *"Worst day of my life."*

Ghini thinks the boy's about to start crying, but he manages to hold it all back, determined to finish telling his story. "But yeah . . . It weren't an exciting escape. It was pitch black, I remember. Clouds blotted the stars, and the moon was empty. But I ran until I couldn't run. Then I walked until I couldn't walk. Then I crawled until I couldn't do that and had to sleep in a hollowed-out tree. There, I woke to a grey and cloudy morning.

"As if waiting on me, the skies opened as I began walking. It wasn't long before I found the road and flagged down a car. Old guy and his wife. They'd heard the local news report a missing kid. But he doesn't think that it's me. He starts calling me 'son,' and I know he isn't thinking twice about this kid in front of him being the missing little girl.

"Though, *she* knew. The old bird did. She'd seen, what I would later in that washroom. Back then, I dressed the part enough. Part of me *always* knew who I was. I just y'know — never mind, it ain't important to you." Ghini wants to grab his inexhaustible hands but restrains herself.

"Anyhow, he thinks I'm a different kid. I roll with it. Make up a sob story bout runnin' way. Show him the injuries, and regardless what the lady thinks, they both convinced now. Eventually made my way down here to Interior, found some work, been here since." He gestures to the church surrounding them.

Samuel passes the flask once more, with a nod communicating gratitude in Clemens-speak.

"So what do I do now? If this cult or whatever has Jeannie, what can I do?" Ghini's at a loss. She wholeheartedly believes the boy but doesn't know where to go from here. "They sound like they could have been doing this for years. Did you ever figure out what they drugged you with or why they took you?"

Bernie shoots to his feet. "Listen, lady. Whether or not you want to hear it. You heard it! So fucking listen! These bitches are straight-up monsters. Not like psychos and serial killers! Like fucking werewolves, zombies, vampires! *MONSTERS!*" He screams the word hopping down from the dais. "If they got ya girl, and she been gone this long, *she — is — dead.* Deal with it, and move on. *Far, far away.* To somewhere cold."

No one has ever gotten away with talking to her like that about Jeannie. She knows better, but she desperately wants to strike him. Connect all her knuckles with his face till the rage is gone.

That ain't you. Anymore.

Before she can listen to herself, she's on her feet too, barely holding back the beast in her chest. "Listen. Thank you. I get that shit's tough. See though, that's my *likkle* girl out there. I don't give a shit what you *think* might have her. I'ma get her back."

Bernie mutters something inaudible, but before Ghini can interpret, it dawns on her.

"I'm sorry. I don't want to invalidate ya. But let me aks you this. Why somewhere cold?"

His green eyes have their own coldness to them as he looks at her, "I don't think *they* like cold. All monsters got somethin', ya know? Vampires got garlic, werewolves got silver bullets; with these things, it's cold. *I think.* They huddle in piles to sleep. We're talking, four, five, six grown men curled up round one lady. Everywhere ya look. I ain't even bother ta count 'em all. But I tell you what, the women's warmth must've been priority. As soon as night fell, the last of 'em ladies came in, and they were immediately piled upon and went to sleep."

Samuel, for the first time, speaks. Though, it's hardly more than a whisper.

"Like bugs."

9

BOYS NOT ALLOWED

"Well, would you lookie here gents? We got us a pair-uh bunnies hiking The Hills." All four men turn to the two women approaching their campsite.

To Queenie and Kari, it appears that for the men, the day has just begun. One has the beginnings of a fire smoldering, while two others muddle about watching. The last man is off to the side with a tiny butane grill, making coffee.

"Excuse Landon. He's got about as much people skills as a pissed-off goose." The men all laugh, except the one that must be Landon. He's pale and plain looking with a nondescript expression on his face, despite the laughter at his expense.

The apologetic man extends a hand directed toward Queenie. "I'm Brandon."

Kari watches as her mother snubs the gesture before fluttering her gaze from one onlooker to the next, wary of each one.

"Hi. I'm Queenie and this is Kari." It comes out matter-of-factly as she glides away from the extended hand.

Brandon has a wry smile that says he is well aware of how the neat rows of teeth look amidst his good bone structure. The awareness of favorable genetics sets Kari on edge. His square jaw perfectly dotted with manicured stubble does anything but entice her or her mother.

Unfazed, he continues. "We're out here for a guys' trip. Every spring like clockwork. Though it's only the single ones making it these days." Kari catches a wink in her periphery. "But hey, we got our boy Landon back!"

Kari pities the men. A bunch of sad, unloved fools, certainly too old to be proud of their loneliness.

"Yeah in exchange for Charlie, and I'd undo that trade in a heartbeat." One of the other men caws.

A boisterous laugh explodes from Brandon's obtuse jaw.

Kari looks first at the small man brewing coffee. He's not laughing and refuses to make eye contact with either Queenie or Kari. Then there's the guy sitting between Brandon and Landon. He's pale and out of shape, with a pristinely shaved head contrasting the dark wooly mass of beard on his chin.

"Sorry about that girls. Tristan's a bit of an ass before coffee o'clock." Brandon adds with a hard slap to his neighbor's back, identifying the jokester. Queenie and Kari lock eyes while Brandon playfully whispers, "he's really a big ole softy. Don't let the gruff beard fool ya."

Tristan's retort is so quiet that both women are sure none of the men are capable of hearing it. *"Two tours of Afghanistan, one of Iraq. Show you softie."*

As the men bicker like children, Queenie moves to the outer edges of the campsite. Her movements are deliberate, as she begins circling the perimeter. A pair of large reflective aviators conceal her eyes from the men for the time being.

Behind her own set, Kari flips her eyes to monitor Queenie's every movement, simultaneously keeping Brandon in her line of sight. Somehow, she's nervous. It seems like an arcane emotion.

"Earth to beautiful, *hello*." Kari twists her neck, giving the appearance of meeting Brandon's sharp blue eyes. *Ice* and *mischief* are the words that come to mind. She glares back, untrusting, hoping the look communicates her irritation.

"Well, that's the kinda glare that'll make a man want to get to know you a bit more—*formally* . . . " He tries to shake *her* hand this time, "Brandon," and just like her mother, Kari wants no part.

The man's presence alone irritates her, but the way he speaks flares up memories of Jason. It's a fleeting image. A past life urging her toward anger. Yet, as quickly as it arrives, a calm rationale eases her emotions.

His fat fingers slide through the back of thinning, dirty-blonde hair with an accompanying laugh. It all feels rehearsed.

"No worries, personal space and all that. Why don't you grab a sit-down and enjoy some breakfast with us? *Most important meal of the day*." He speaks to them as if the tidbit, along with his angular jawline, can convince the pair of them.

Queenie can tell that Kari is looking to her for guidance, as the big man continues to irritate her daughter. But Kari will have to wait. Queenie's attention is intent on the bearded one. He's pulling a pair of large coolers to the fire. Each leaving deep trenches in the dirt. Satisfied, she meets her daughter's gaze.

All her mother offers is a nod. A gesture instructing her to hold tight a bit longer. Brandon interprets the motion as well and slides a hand to the small of Kari's back. While it is an unwelcome touch, the movement is gentle and guiding.

But it doesn't stay that way.

His fingers ease a revolting pressure toward her waistline.

A loud *crkckcrkckk* rings amongst the group.

It's an old nervous tick of Kari's to crack her neck. It's silly for her to be nervous. She channels her rage into the imagery of grabbing and snapping Brandon's wrist with the same sort of crunch. The sound flutters through her imagination, filling her with calming euphoria as she takes a seat.

While Queenie finishes her inspection, Kari catches herself in Queenie's glasses. A mischievous smile curls at the corners of her fulsome lips. Returning the grin, her mother squeezes in between Kari and Brandon.

Sat next to the square-jawed man, Queenie smells a forced scent. Artificial pine. Unnatural in its deception. Queenie distrusts the man even more than she already had.

"Coffee?" The small shy one asks, approaching with two mugs in hand. There were twelve-year-olds bigger than this puny man. His self-worth is even more pitiful as he slumps his shoulders, dejected, at both women's stoic refusal. Tail between his legs, he heads back to his picnic table to busy himself with the glowing screen of a cellphone.

Queenie continues to take the group in.

A bunch of Nowheresville white boys. The only one of interest is Square Jaw. Something emanates from him. Disrupting the air around her.

Emotional reverberations of the night her mother had taken her through an alleyway as a shortcut. Where a man had emerged from the shadows. But Queenie had *known*. She'd known someone was there before they set foot in that alley. She'd gripped her mother's hand so tightly, dragging her through the sickly space with as much strength as an eight-year-old could muster.

Though, this time, the sensation excites her.

"So what say you?" Brandon looks at Queenie with cloud-less sky-colored eyes.

"Sorry, I wasn't paying attention to *you*." A flat spitefulness nips at the end of her sentence.

"Oh you ladies, always the same. Never living in the moment. Probably, thinking about some way to argue with, let me guess, a baby daddy back home." This time it's the ordinary one. The only thing that stands out about him is dull red hair peaking beneath a beanie.

"Lay off man." The little guy pipes up from his island. "I'm sure she's just bored with the conversation. Most women don't want to talk about huntin'." She notices a bit of a drawl in him, and for a moment Queenie finds it endearing to the little guy. "Girls is always too delicate for huntin' 'nd blood 'nd guts. 'Ch'is why they more suited to the kitch'n, once the real dirty work's b'in d'un."

She no longer finds the tiny man endearing.

Queenie's eyes focus back on Square Jaw as his foul-smelling cracked lips gravitate toward her ear. There's little room to inch away, and what she can manage doesn't deter his approach.

"If you don't have a man back home, hell, even if you do, I'd be happy to show ya why the ladies always call me, White Chocolate. If you know what I mean? My Nubian Queen."

His hand slides over her thigh, and every nerve ending tenses at his touch, yet it fails to give him pause for his actions.

She's done with them all.

He whispers something revolting again, but Queenie refuses to listen.

Kari can sense something's wrong, and her focus zooms toward her mother, whose glasses have lowered to the bridge of her nose.

"What the *fuck* is wrong with your —" There's an airy grunt as Brandon's body goes slack, nearly teetering into the fire.

The group's attention swings to Queenie and Brandon. She's whispering something into his ear now. With a sickening jello-like *slurp*, Queenie's index finger rises, pointed, and dripping a steady rhythm of crimson.

"Kill them."

There's a deep stain pooling on Brandon's thigh as he stands.

"Brandon. Dude, what'd she do to you?" Whimpers the ordinary man.

Brandon's taller than either woman had realized now that he is on his feet. But it's his eyes that stand out to Kari most. They've lost their hue, fading into a milky silver.

Square Jaw moves awkwardly, almost drunk, lurching toward the ordinary man opposite the fire. Surprisingly, the big man doesn't sidestep. He plants his foot straight into the fire without a second thought. His large mitts quickly engage the nondescript man on the other side.

While his friends lock against one another, the soldier sprints to a tent, only to emerge swiftly with the flourish of a butterfly knife. Strangely, he doesn't engage. As if he's waiting his turn. Instead, he stands waiting, baring stained teeth through his grizzly beard like a cornered badger.

Still, there's not much he could do to deter Square Jaw. The large man stands hunched, fingers curled around Plain Man's throat, while the knuckles of his other fist slammed into the man's face with lifeless thuds.

The small one has dropped under the picnic table, fetal, and shielding his head like it's an elementary school tornado drill.

Once Plain Man stills, Square Jaw's grip goes slack. He wastes no time dropping the lifeless body into the dirt. His clothing and face are covered in spray, while the motionless man lay purple-faced in the dust. Battered and bloodied, he'd be unrecognizable to friends and family.

Already, Square Jaw is on top of Knife Man. Unlike the first man, the soldier doesn't hesitate to slash at his friend. Swipe after swipe tears at Square Jaw's flesh, yet he never flinches. He presses his looming size forward. Knife Man, on the other hand, looks tired and weary as anger burns through his pale skin.

Just then, a desperate thrust manages to pierce Brandon's abdomen. Envy envelops Kari, wishing she had been the one to do it. Though, she knows the wound will do little to stop her mother's pet.

Sure enough, he grabs the now unarmed man by the wrist, and with a swift whip, the bearded man's ulna erupts through his skin. The knife still protrudes from Brandon's side as he digs thick fingers into the soldier's mangy beard. With ease, he then hoists the man upward into the trunk of a tree with a violent heave. The man's throat doesn't stand a chance between the force of Brandon's hand and the thick trunk. A sickening burst lingers in the air as the dead man's eyes roll to the back of his skull.

"Kari?"

"Yes, mother." She perks up at the sound of her name.

"You want this one, don't you?"

"More than anything."

"Then he is yours."

For the first time, Queenie gets to watch her daughter hunt. Kari's speed is rapid. Her feet flutter across the dirt with little more than a hum. The sound of ribs cracking and skin bursting echoes loudly into the woods.

The large man dangles limply on her forearm. "*Damn.* I didn't mean for it to be that quick." She grabs Brandon's limp wrist, using it as the fulcrum to slide the corpse from her arm.

The viscera is warm, but the morning air sends chills through her soaked sleeve.

In a fog of lustful wrath, she snaps the dead man's wrist, before casting the lifeless mass to the side.

"Kari. My dear daughter, there's still one left."

The mortifying gaffe fuels her rage. The little one is crawling away on all fours and it's clear that he hears them. Attempting to get to his feet, he stumbles.

Meanwhile, Kari reaches for Brandon's lifeless form. There's an intoxicating strength in her hand as she squeezes the bones and ligaments of his ankle. They compress and roll under her fingertips as she flings the body like it were a sack of trash to a dumpster.

The dripping corpse arcs through the air, before crashing into the tiny one's back. The collision sends him spinning headfirst into a large pine.

With deadly grace, the two women stride over to the sad little wretch, who lay twitching on the ground, very much alive. The sight of blood pulsing out of his forehead confirms it. Both Kari and her mother study him the way a torturous child studies an ant before incinerating it with a magnifying glass.

The man's legs don't seem to work. He's slowly coming to. His fingers know to dig through the dusty earth. Anything to crawl and move as far as possible.

"I think we need to put him down, sweet Kari." There's a somber glee to Queenie's words.

Kari feels that she owes this to her mother. This time, she acts with deliberate speed and force. She eyes the back of his head, before slamming her boot heel, popping the insignificant man's skull with more ease than a teen pops a zit.

"Thank you, my dear. Let's grab one of the tents and roll them up in it. Then grab another and roll up their belongings."

"Do we not want to grab the last two tents?"

Queenie thinks about it. Walter's words were ingrained into her mind. *You are not invincible. You are strong. You are durable. But you are killable. So —*

"You are so wise, sweet Kari. We must not leave a trace here, we must always — *proceed with caution.*"

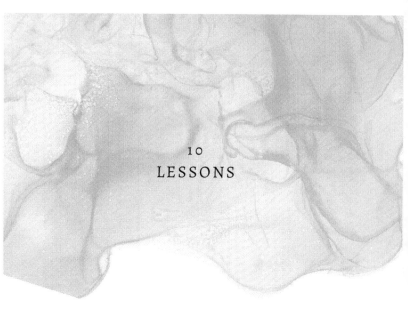

1 0

LESSONS

"**Y**ou can't blame him."

"I don't." Samuel says amid smacks of nicotine gum. It fills the cab with an off-putting spearmint scent.

"Then why are you acting so, I don't know, *frustrated?*" To be fair, she's not entirely sure that's the appropriate word for his behavior. However, she's ridden plenty with Samuel this past year, and, right now, he's driving in silence. He never drives in silence. He's always got something on the radio.

"I blame you." He says, not letting his eyes drift from the road.

"What do you mean, you blame *me?*" She regrets raising her voice. "*Sorry, Samuel.*"

"Don't bother, 's'all forgiven. Family goes hand in hand with emotion." He pops a second piece of gum, while deftly operating the wheel with his knees. "Listen. There's a lot I know about that fella there. He is family after all."

She's not sure where he's going with this. "I get that, but—

"

"Please Ghini. I don' do it much, but I need ta be the one ta talk."

She looks at him wide-eyed. Ghini doesn't have a lot of respect for most people she meets, which she knows is a character flaw, but there's certainly no one she respects more than Samuel. He's been her father figure for this phase of her life, and if he's going to ask for her patience, it's the least she can do.

"Thank ya. Listen, I don't mind ya not understanding a lot of what's going on here. But the way ya left things — it weren't fair ta Bern."

"What do you mean?"

"Ya don't trust the boy."

Samuel's keeping to the speed limit on purpose. He wants to talk this through with her. "Why would you even say that?" Defensiveness leaks out from her voice. It's a reflex. A coping mechanism. She'll always protect herself if she feels the least bit threatened. It's the only way she knows how to survive.

"Listen Ghini. Yer a kind woman. I know ya. Ya worked hard to be kind to Bern after he finished his story, but ya wasn't bein' *genuine*." That word. They had a history with that word. "Ya was placatin' the boy."

"He's barely a boy!" Shame and regret assault her mind before the words depart her lips. "I'm sorry." Embarrassment, and subsequently, worthlessness, quiet the beast in her chest. It's that damn word — *genuine*.

She hears him though. "You're right. And I know better. I do. I'm just — I don't know. It's all just so — ?"

"Hard to believe." He finishes the thought for her.

"*Yeah.*" A heavy silence sits on the bench seat between them. "So, it's my fault Bernie didn't come back with us. Cuz I didn't believe him?" Ghini's words resonate like a universal truth.

"Check the ego. He's smart, he knows you don't believe him. But, that ain't why."

"Okay. So, he's afraid. But how am I supposed to believe that some sort of — *bug-vampire* — has taken my little girl?"

"Yer missing' the point. Do ya believe in the Lord?"

She thinks about that. She *did*. It's hard to say anymore. The church no longer feels welcoming. Too many eyes. Too many questions. But does that mean she doesn't believe?

Honor God In All We Do

The words flash behind her eyes, and she can't bring herself to say she doesn't, but — "Faith's been tested."

"As is faith's nature. Can't be faith if there ain't a test." She thinks about this but doesn't see the train of thought. Then he adds, "If ya can have faith in the Lord. Why can't ya have faith that we don't fully understand this world? That monsters may be more than imagination?"

She's feeling the fury associated with her walls going up. She feels angry at being questioned. It all becomes about her as she struggles to fight off the urge to argue with the man. *But how dare he compare the lord to a monster?* She thought he was a man of God himself.

"Listen. That face says yer *still* missin' the point. This is bout taking faith and applying it to trust."

"No. Hold on. Do you believe in the Bogeyman, Sam?"

"Not in the conventional sense, no." He says, cooly.

"But you believe in these *bug people?*"

"There's evidence ain't there. I mean, we're a Dinosaur state, can't be saying there ain't no Dinos when you can dig up one in ya backyard. Which is why —"

"There's no evidence Samuel." She has to cut him off. Talkative Samuel is not her favorite person at this moment. "There's a boy. A boy, Samuel! How old is he anyways? Never mind, doesn't matter. Point is, he's alone and prob'ly scared.

And he prob'ly concocted the whole damn story just to come to terms with what *really* happened out in those woods. Who's to say it wasn't because he was scared to transition at home, around prying eyes? I ain't got no problem with no transitions, but that boy, he's scared. And he's got no family to care for 'em." There she goes, another step backward. Every time she lets that beast's wrath loose, even a tiny bit, it gets the best of her.

Sam glides the car to the shoulder. They're still a ways from Rapid City. The only sights for miles are empty golden prairies and the mounds that mark The Badlands shrinking in the distance.

"Listen here. That's my kin. I love that boy with all my heart, and I trust him." There's a father-like sternness in his eyes.

Likely why he pulled off, just to give me that look.

"Now. I tried to care for that boy after his mother — my sister, mind — done and offed herself. When he'd found out. We lost all contact. We knew he was in Interior," he says it like *eN-teer-ya*. "But by the time we got there he'd flown the coop, and I'd feared the worst. Then, about a month later we find him wanderin' the hills. He'd run back there lookin' for death, but couldn't find it, couldn't do it hisself neether. Thankfully.

"I tried to give him a home, but he couldn't stick it. Not in the heart of the hills. He wouldn't sleep for weeks, not really. Wouldn't leave the house. Barely ate or drank anything that didn't contain caffeine or sugar."

She sees a different look in his eyes. It remains fatherly, only it's not that disapproving glare. He's pleading for her to understand.

"I ain't trying to guilt trip ya. The transition has been hard enough on the boy, but what's even harder, are these memories. He's told me that story a dozen times. It don't change.

Kids always changing they stories. They want it to suit they point exactly. Bern ain't changed that story once in almost *ten years*. And you of all people'd know — I'd remember if he did."

She's shocked by the number.

Ten years.

It stands out to her, but she can't place it. Regardless, she knows he's right. With Samuel's memory as it was, he'd know. Ghini also realizes he's not much of a boy anymore. A decade on his own would certainly make an adult of anyone.

"Get out ya own way here Ghini. Look at this as objectively as ya can. Think back to what we was just talking about. *Trust*."

She remembers the boy's scars, not just the ones on his shoulder. But there had been others she'd seen. The kinds that screamed *self-harm*. She knows that's a difficult situation in the LGBTQ+ community. She recalls the vividness of the boy's tale. *Kids do have overactive imaginations, especially around trauma though.*

"Did he always seem like he was going to be transgender?"

"What's that matter?"

She's embarrassed to say where her mind's going. "I just wonder . . ."

"I'll stop ya. Don't wonder. We ain't talked much bout it. Clemens way, I 'spose. But, I tell ya this. That was an adventurous rugrat with little fear in they bones and never a drop in they eyes. Then when we brought him home, he was borderline agoraphobic. Couldn't get him outta the house. Immediately started dressing in baggier clothes than was normal. And in public, wouldn't speak with anything but a forced baritone to his voice. Before all that though, he done chopped off all his hair. What you saw today, that's the longest I'd seen it in years."

Ghini notices Samuel's gaze has gone out the window. He's

no longer looking at her, and it seems the lines of his tanned fuzzy face have creased into canyons during the time they'd sat here.

"Whatever happened out there changed that kid's life in a way that can't be undone." He takes a deep breath. "Listen well Ghini. Belief, faith, and trust . . . all three are things that're incredibly different, but get mixed up. You can choose to believe in something like God or monsters. You can have faith that God looks out for you, and that locking yer door keeps ya safe from the monsters.

"Trust is different. You trust the clergy to guide your faith, not because they have to, but because they want to. You trust that the silver bullet does the trick against the monster, not because you have to, but because that's how others tell you they stopped it before you.

"If you don't want to believe Bernie, well that's yours to decide, but I tell you what, there's plenty of this world that we don't understand. Yet, all us adults got a parental instinct. One that's programmed into us through evolution. And this old man's instincts believe that kid. I have faith that he is a good man and wouldn't try to dupe me like that. But most importantly, I trust him with my life.

"You don't go to war standing next to somebody you can't trust. And when you *can* trust 'em, you can put your faith in them, and when you have faith in something or *someone*, it makes believing 'em a whole lot easier."

As silence permeates throughout the cab. Samuel pushes the car into drive, easing it back onto the highway. The sun is almost at the center of the windshield. Its blinding glare forces Ghini to look out the window. As the prairie whizzes past, she's left to think about Bernie. All alone out there. Living those precious teenage years in hiding. Ten years. *Going through something so difficult.*

Alone.

An old conversation echoes its remnants within Ghini's mind.

'MOMMY? *Why are those people being mean to that man?'*

She'd been watching the news. A story about a black man, beaten and bound by his neighbors because his description vaguely matched a man wanted for murder. Turns out the murderer was already in custody. Had been for a day. News just ain't report it. Ain't nothing happen to those men.

'Listen here my likkle buttercup.' She pulled, a then five-year-old Jeannie onto her lap. Her voluptuous curls balled onto either side of her head. She wanted to look like Minnie Mouse in her red and white polka dot dress. She recalls how heavy Jeannie was, and wondered how much longer she'd have before her little girl wouldn't want to sit on her lap anymore.

'You are a black woman in America, and your life won't be easy. But you have to be kind. Those people there aren't being very kind to that man cuz they mommas never sat them down like this. Now, there are gonna be some who have it harder than you. They gonna make decisions different than your own, but we have to love all God's creatures the same, especially those struggling. People gonna make it hard for you to trust them, but don't let the bad ones taint that trust cuz it'll just make you an enemy of yourself.'

"WHY WOULD a kid put themselves through all of that?" She asks herself out loud. "A young girl, in *South Dakota*, no less. Leaves her home as a teenager to transition to being a boy, in a church, in a rural town that hardly has running water and electricity. They'd have to be pretty motivated?"

It's a rhetorical question. Nonetheless, Samuel offers an affirmative grunt.

The pair of them stew amongst their thoughts for some time, and Ghini replays the day in her mind.

"I'm sorry Samuel." The words are growing old, but that's one thing her grandma taught her above all else.

Apologize as soon as ya can, cuz you never want someone to leave this world not knowing two things. That you love them, and you sorry if you hurt them.

"I trust *you.* So, I know I can trust Bernie. I just . . . How am I 'sposed to go to Dak, and say, I think *monsters* have my baby girl?"

"Never said ya should. Not yet. He's a man who needs data and physical evidence. He can operate off a gut feeling from time ta time, but that job ain't gonna let him do anything like this without evidence."

"Okay. So, what about the video?"

"Video is video. It ain't perfect. He'll need more n' that."

"Then what next?"

"We prepare."

"For what?"

"For the inevitable encounter." Samuel spits out his gum into an old coffee-stained mug. "We'll have to do somethin' bout the cold. It's almost summer." He turns off the ramp into the outskirts of Rapid City.

"It's barely spring."

"Even worse. Now we may get one last surprise snow, but I just doubt that. Our luck ain't that good. So, if it's bout to be any season, it's gonna be the season of the monster, and should we encounter 'em, we'll need a plan."

A plan. That's all she can think about until Samuel drops

her off at the shambley apartment complex that she now calls home. Samuel says he'll be in touch, but he's got shift work the next day, so she'll have to come to the bar in the evening if she needs anything.

Inside her apartment, she's left to mull through the entirety of the day. A thousand-yard stare envelops her. None of it makes sense to Ghini, and she's not sure how she can make it make sense.

Then it dawns on her.

On the wall is a picture, well a cross-stitch of a picture she'd made with her grandmother when Ghini was just a girl. It was of a black woman in a victorian dress reading a book. She's sat in a luxurious, high-backed, green armchair. All these years later, Ghini had kept it so she could remember the good part of that day.

But, what it reminds her of now is not the day or the unfortunate tragedy that awaited them upon coming home, but where they'd gotten the supplies — *the library*. Back in those days when they supported such hobbies and activities. The design was a mimic of a painting on the library's wall. Except a little Ghini wanted the woman in her beautiful yellow dress to look like her, so that's exactly what she and her grandmother did.

It was too late now. The library wasn't doing well and it'd be well closed at this hour. Thankfully it opened at nine the next morning, and she could be there first thing. Until then, she'd try to sleep. It'd been a couple of days since she'd done that successfully.

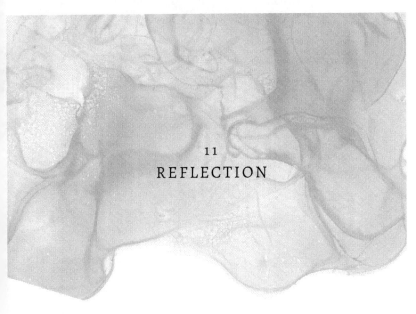

11
REFLECTION

I nside their cave, it's humid and warm. They had both felt a feverish chill sneaking up on them as they returned home. It had been a busy day, and significantly longer than they'd intended.

Now that the sun has set, both women feel fatigued and exhausted. Thankfully their stomachs are full as they continue to warm themselves around a fire. Huddling for the heat from each other's bodies under a comforter, they teeter on the verge of sleep.

Kari nestles into Queenie's curvy waistline, while her mother wraps her arms around her. There's a comforting strength to the steel girders that Queenie calls arms. Feeling safe, Kari rests her head against her mother's shoulder.

In return, Queenie feels a growing instinct to support this darling child, whom she knows would do anything for her. She wants more of this. She wants more daughters, enough to share the entirety of her love.

She looks back to the wall of muddy bulges, knowing she will have what she desires soon enough.

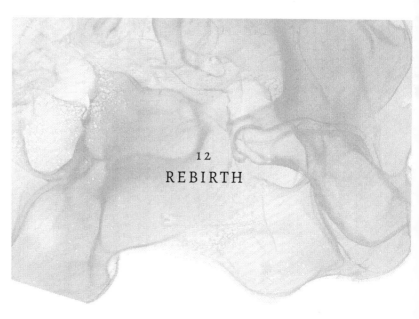

12
REBIRTH

The flames flicker an energizing strength into both women as they patiently wait beside their morning fire.

Queenie hears the sound first.

thudup-thudup-thudupthudup-thudupthudup.

The speedy beat pulses faster and louder, pulling Kari's attention away from the last bits of breakfast wedged between her teeth. Meanwhile, her mother's smile shines like pearls, as joy consumes her face. Elation springboards Queenie to her feet at the first sight of a hand breaking through its muddy entombment.

"Our *likkle* family grows my sweet Kari!" She extends a hand, pulling Kari to her feet with ease. They watch as the first woman emerges.

"Wh—where am I?" The woman stutters. She stumbles over the remnants of her chrysalis. Fortunately, both Kari and Queenie are there to catch her. Kari grabs a comforter to help warm her new sister. She recalls how cold the air had been on her flesh when she'd emerged.

"It's okay my dear. You are safe, you are home, you are with family!" Queenie exclaims and dances away in a twirl, leaving Kari to assist their newest arrival toward the fire. They snuggle her up in a canvas chair.

Thanks, Brandon.

"I was. I was." She mutters more but it's incoherent gibberish.

Kari can't recall this much confusion. She wonders if the woman's age — Kari thinks fifties — has something to do with it. She'd also been a bit heavy-set. Though, the assimilation has affected her the same way it had Kari. Most of that excess adipose tissue in the woman's face and abdomen has melted away. She has a Jane Lynch sort of look to her with a strong jaw, high cheekbones, and short platinum hair.

"It's okay, the memories come and go at first. They'll eventually flood back, but you won't need them. You're my sister now. I'm here for you." Kari crouches at her sister's side, hooks an arm around her, and rests her head on the woman's shoulder. With joy, she watches her sister's eyes flutter from a vibrant amber brown to a honeycomb of color and pupils.

"Sister?" The woman's brow furrows tightly as if the thought pains her.

Queenie glides toward her two daughters, her heart pulsing with joy to feed her newborn. She has already gone and fetched a plastic plate of raw meat, and a cheap cup filled with apple juice.

"The juice is to get you some sugar. It's good for you." She hands the woman the cup, careful not to spill, amidst her excitement. Her daughter is eager to sip away at the drink. Quenching a vigorous thirst Queenie knows well. "*This* is breakfast. Eat up. You'll need your strength." She adds handing over the plate careful not to drip.

Juicy thigh.

Kari goes to say something, but her mother dismisses her with a shake of her head as if she can read Kari's mind. The woman dives into the dripping meat without hesitation. The second bite follows the first before she's finished chewing. Then a third, and a fourth.

Kari had hesitated, and she now aches with a pang of shame that she hadn't accepted the meal as willingly.

"This is so good." Lynn whispers ravenously.

"It is, isn't it." Queenie feels her heart swell with love for her newborn.

"Queenie?" The woman asks.

"Yes, love?"

"Nothing. I just know that's your name. How do I know? You told me. In the woods." Her eyes flutter. "Kari?" Kari nods. "My *family*."

"Yes, sweet child. *Family*."

Just then, the second chrysalis audibly cracks behind them. Queenie hasn't lost any excitement and wonder for the process. "Kari, please take care of Lynn. I will tend to Melanie."

Kari assumes her responsibility and begins answering the woman's questions. They seem to be the same ones Kari had asked, and though she doesn't have all the answers, it's a relief that her sister accepts each explanation with ease.

Meanwhile, Queenie greets Melanie with childlike glee, as the girl emerges from her slumber. Melanie had looked very much like Lynn, no surprise considering the woman had been her mother. They had shared the same short and squat build, though Mel stood a head shorter. Nonetheless, Queenie recalls a cute young girl before the assimilation. One with squirrelly cheeks and magnificent auburn hair, along with one of those little button noses that turned upward.

Now, her hair was a radiant scarlet. Its vibrance is in stark contrast with the darkness of their space. Strangely, she hasn't shed those squirrelly cheeks, especially considering how her body has adjusted with stunning results. She no longer looked like a girl, her figure has become some women's idyllic pear shape. Similar to Queenie's. Though Melanie's waist appears wider than her mother's, but tiny in comparison to her curvy hips.

"Queenie." She says with a smile that radiates joy through her new mother. Queenie watches the girl's eyes flicker into a honeycomb, but they settle, unlike her two previous daughters' who fluttered back and forth. They're a piercing robin's egg set with a menagerie of pupils. It's hypnotizing and beautiful.

It's an unexpected delight. She hadn't imagined that she'd find an Alpha so soon. There was hope for Kari, but she doesn't need hope for Melanie.

Queenie knows.

"My sweet Melanie." She clutches the girl in her arms, wrapping her tightly in a Star Wars comforter.

In death, those boys have provided us with a bounty.

"Mel."

"What dear?"

"Please mother. Call me Mel."

"Of course my sweet child."

"Mother?" The pair lock eyes. Their honeycombs stare through one another, and it's as if they can communicate in silence.

"Go join Kari and Lynn. I will grab you some food." Queenie kisses Mel on the forehead. She can't help thinking about the girl. She is so small in comparison to her sisters. Everything about her is different.

The thought of what Mel may be capable of is — *exhilarating.*

Kari starts to her feet, quizzically taking in her newest sister's appearance, but Mel's quick to dismiss her with an off-putting gesture. Slowly, she trails over with the comforter draped across her shoulders.

In no time, the three sisters are nestled near one another. Silence has taken hold of them and Kari can't help but notice the difference between herself and Mel. She's worried about her sister. She has concerns that the girl hadn't completed the assimilation before hatching.

"No need to worry so much Kari." Those piercing blue honeycombs scan Kari as if she can X-Ray through her. "I can feel it coming off of you. *The worry.* Why are you so worried, sister of mine?"

There's a snide tone behind those words, which Kari finds distasteful. In return, she can feel her entire body tense. Oh how she'd love to teach the girl a little lesson, she thinks. She'd show her why it's disrespectful to try and get inside her head, to assume what Kari was thinking. This blooms into a full sense of loathing in an instant. It feels violating the way the little runt could almost read her — *no,* she dare not even think such things.

"You look so *similar.* I'm not saying you *haven't* changed, but *clearly* not as much as Lynn or I. I can't help but wonder *why? I just hope you're okay.*" The words fall flat, and Kari's well aware that they both know, that she, in fact, does not care.

"There are many reasons why her assimilation may have been different." Queenie says, returning from the shadows of the tunnels with her newborn's breakfast. "Lots of stuff can contribute to how we change. But Mel's the youngest of you three, which's might be why." She passes the plate to Mel's outstretched hands, and she tears it away from their mother with vicious speed.

"How old are *you*?" Mel asks tritely, speaking through a mouthful of meat. She hadn't even bothered to look it over — even give it a whiff. She's completely ignored the juice altogether.

"I am the oldest!" Queenie says with glee. "It doesn't matter what the number is, just that I am that, and I am the mother to you all." Her gaze meets each of her daughters'. Joy swells under her chest, watching Kari and Lynn's eyes flutter into a honeycomb. Mel's however, have yet to revert back.

"The oldest *of what*, mother?" Mel inquires with that tone that is beginning to grind at Kari's sense of respect for Queenie. The girl is insolent, she thinks. Their mother will tell them when she sees fit. Kari knows instinctually that Mel's eyes are on her, and she tries to bury those feelings as quickly as she can; refusing to let the brat know how she's feeling toward her.

Never again.

"Ah, a great question." Queenie pauses. She will choose her words carefully. This is a new element — dealing with Mel. "We are a *family*. A family brought together across time. Together we will build all of this," she waves her arms, pointing to the many passages leading from their current chamber, "into a home. As one, we will bloom. Just like flowers! And we're gonna hunt for the best flowers! Or, uhm, sisters. Yup sisters!"

Queenie has a lot to learn still, she is a bit embarrassed with her lack of speaking skills, but no one in her family ever really had any to begin with.

"Why are there no men?" It's Lynn this time, but she is meek and respectful to their mother. *Unlike her daughter.* It dawns on Kari that neither of them has acknowledged the familial relationship, though they seem to have no problem treating one another as siblings.

"We do not need them. All our sisters and daughters need is their mother. So we find them, bring them here, and free them."

"Free them, from what?" Mel's quick to interject, shooting a sly look in Kari's direction.

Queenie's lips pucker and she taps at her chin in thought. She isn't sure what to say here. Walter said she would know when she was ready to explain. *Was she ready?* She hadn't been with Kari, but Mel makes her think she is.

Then again . . .

"Free them from a world that doesn't benefit them. From a world that takes advantage of women and girls. That makes them weaker, not stronger. From the poor decisions of selfish mothers and absent fathers."

Kari notices the spite leaching through her mother's words. Unfortunately, it is Mel who reaches out a hand first. She takes Queenie's gently between the slender fingers of her dainty palms. "It's okay Mother. We can learn more of our purpose later."

Queenie's tension eases with a nod, "Our purpose is to grow our colony to be strong." She no longer wants to answer questions and abruptly wanders off toward the mouth of the cave, letting Mel's hand fall from hers. "Kari."

"Yes, Mother." She is excited to be addressed.

"Please, prep your sisters for the day. They need clothes and to be taught the rules. Then meet me outside. We continue to grow our family today."

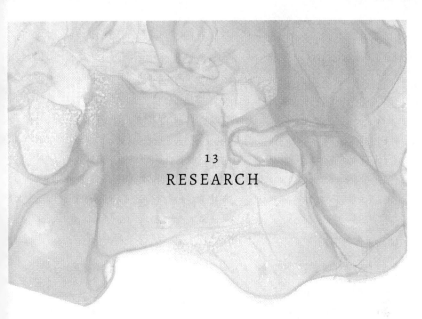

13
RESEARCH

Ghini can't remember the last time she'd gone to the library. She would have been just a girl. It's no longer the grubby, old, yellow-tinted prison that she remembers. It has character. A modern aesthetic and clean environment.

Hence, why it likely had its struggles. Too much money out, not enough coming in.

There are several large computer banks with public access to wi-fi, which is all she needs. Near the closest set, they've installed a miniature coffee counter. Behind, stands a tiny Hispanic woman busying herself with the morning's tasks. Ghini thinks about a coffee, but she's itching at the bit to dive into those keys and find anything that might help her.

As a girl, the majority of her experiences here were thanks to after-school programs. Her father had to work doubles most nights, and her grandmother had to work to support her own daughter, Ghini's mother, as she weaseled her way in and out of rehab.

Back then Ghini, herself, had been more concerned with

sneaking off to meet Vikki M and Vickey S to smoke ciga-
rettes behind the dumpster.

She chuckles to herself, somewhat missing those days.
Sure they had always gotten into trouble, but Ghini remem-
bers it fondly. Though, she'd promised herself she'd never let
Jeannie live that kind of life — even if they both had a mother
who'd needed rehab. At least for Ghini, it had taken after the
one stint. Thankfully Jeannie had been too young to
remember.

Well for the cocaine it'd taken.

Booze, Adderal, and weed were a recent step backward.

All things in moderation. If only Vikki M had known that.

Ghini'd gone to visit Vickey S just last year at the women's
prison and heard about Vikki M's OD. Ghini's lost a lot of
people over the years, and she needs to make sure that she
doesn't add Jeannie to that list. She knows deep down that her
baby girl is alive. She just has to find her, and nothing will
stop her from doing just that.

She pulls up a seat at a nice new PC and tries to covertly
pop an Adderall. Instant release. She needs the amphetamine
for its actual purpose now — to focus. She scours Google for
things like *Monster Bugs, Bug Monsters, Black Hills Rare Bugs,
Human Infections From Bugs*, but there's nothing promising.

Time flies while she is consumed with her searches, franti-
cally clicking through images of cartoon monsters, horren-
dous rashes and infections, not to mention a multitude of
entomology catalogs — which she learns is the study of bugs.
Most of the images send shivers down her spine. Enlarged
views of real and drawn pincers that could slice through a
man by the looks of it. Antennae with hairs thick as a horse's
mane, and eyes — *wait.*

Eyes.

She pulls out her phone and looks at the picture of The

Dop — as she's started calling her — too afraid to assign the woman the name she is certain belongs to her. The woman's eyes are blurry, and difficult to make out. Ghini had written it off as a distortion, but now they remind her of all the leopard-spotted clothing she owns. She searches, *leopard eyes.*

Nothing but leopards.

Spotted eyes.

She finds plenty of pictures of people with little brown freckles in the color part of their eyes, but there's nothing like what she's pulled up on her phone. She needs to find eyes with lots of dots — whatever they're called — and no white, only color.

That's a place to start, she reckons. Figure out what the terms are.

A quick skim of Google hits her with a crash course: *irises — the color,* and *pupils — the dot.*

Eyes with multiple pupils.

This search gets her closer.

She's not sure if some of the images are real but they make her cringe nonetheless. Many are hard to look at. It's like the iris part of the eye is torn open in different spots, forming all these abnormal pupils. But they all still have white in their eyes. She looks away from the screen, her stomach churns in a way that makes her think about leaving this tract behind, but she tells herself she's too strong for that. Even if she retches, Ghini knows to keep going. She knows her baby needs her.

Her eyes have drifted away from the computer for an unknown amount of time. She has let her mind wander, concerned with where she should go from here. Then, in an instant, something dawns on her.

She needs to combine her searches. She has been going about it all wrong.

Insects with many pupils.

She now knows that's the proper term as well — not bugs. Now she's getting somewhere.

There are moths and dragonflies and all sorts of insects that she doesn't know the names of. The blown-up images fill her screen but aren't as unsettling to look at. Especially the one. It stands out immediately. The butterfly. Its eyes look almost identical to The Dop's.

Another search, a few clicks, and Ghini discovers something that chills her. It's a bit of folklore that sounds oddly familiar, yet alien. She begins reading myths of the Russian *Baba Yaga* on a site titled "Hoax or Horror." The article she's found is specifically labeled, *"Butterfly monsters and myths."*

They also refer to it as the *babochka*, which she learns is Russian for butterfly. So, Ghini does a deep dive throughout the internet to learn more about the witchey-bogey-monster of Russian lore. The creature eats children and is depicted most often as being gruesome and grotesque, but very much human. She is often surrounded by a posse of women servants. But the *Baba Yaga's* eyes, every image she finds, they're always human. Not once are they drawn with these multiple pupils.

An alarm goes off on her phone. It's 1:45. She needs to start wrapping things up if she is to get out of here on time and catch the 2:15 bus to work. She decides that coffee and stretching her legs might do her some good before she has to head out to — *honor God in all the coke bottles.*

"What ya working on ma'am?" The tiny barista asks while preparing Ghini's Americano.

"Just some research."

"Well of course. That's what the library's for! But what are ya researching?"

Ghini is embarrassed to say. Except, she's well aware that her screen's been visible to anyone standing at the coffee counter. Considering how empty the place has been, she does not doubt that the barista had spent time looking over Ghini's shoulder noticing her unusual search history. She decides to settle on a half-truth.

"Insects."

"Ah, yes. Insects. They are always coming back this time of year. Such interesting creatures. Pollinating and furthering life. But also violent. And territorial to boot. Thinking they can invade and co-op space, calling it their own."

She clicks the lid atop the steaming coffee and passes it to Ghini. The warmth in her hands feels good against her chilly fingertips. Maybe poor circulation, she worries about familial history. "Thank you."

The barista nods and wishes her luck.

Back at the PC, Ghini goes to close everything out and collect her things, when she sees a note resting on the keyboard.

You're looking in the wrong place. Scribbled in a sloppy, sloping hand, as if they'd tried to write diagonally across the page.

There on her screen is not the *Baba Yaga*, but a close-up picture of an insect's eye. She reads the caption.

Pseudopupils are common to many families of insects including moths, butterflies, and several species of wasps.

She scans the room and there are a few people scattered about, but there's no telling who left the note. One thing is certain though. They're willing to talk. There's a phone number scrawled on the back of the message. Though, it's not an area code she can say she's familiar with.

14

DROPPED

T he street lamps seem to flicker past as she stares
down at the ten digits scrawled with a mysterious
hand. No part of the number triggers any sense of
familiarity.

The area code — 309. She googles it. Illinois. There's not a
single person Ghini can think of from Illinois. Not even the
rare extended family member, past participant from *The Real,*
or anyone comes to mind.

So, why does she have this number? And, who gave it to
her? But most importantly — who will be picking up the line
when Ghini dials it?

Her phone says 11:52 pm. It's a bit late to call, but *screw it,*
she thinks. This is about finding Jeannie, so there's no reason
not to try the number that has been burning a hole in her
pocket and her mind throughout the entire day.

She hovers a thumb over the green dial button for a
second, but not a beat more. She slams it down and guides the
device to her ear. Nervously, she listens to the rings that feel

more foreboding than usual. They stretch on for what seems an eternity. The noise echoes itself.

Ring.

Ring.

Ring.

Just when she's about ready to give up hope, the line connects. The other end is eerily silent. She checks that the call hasn't dropped.

"Hello?" Ghini's meek voice inquires warily.

Still, silence permeates the line.

She repeats herself. *"Hello?"*

"Who thees?" A woman's voice comes through with a strong Hispanic accent.

"Um. Yes, did you leave this number on my table at the library?"

"Is this a sort of prank?"

"Prank?" Was this a *prank?* Had she been tricked into a crank phone call? This is where the old Ghini would hang up. So, she knows to continue. This woman may have what she needs. No. She is *supposed* to have the answers, she tells herself. "No ma'am. It ain't a prank. I'm sorry it's late and all, but, uh, I'm in South Dakota, Rapid City specifically." That odd silence creeps back into the other side of the line, but they're still there. Ghini checks. "And — I, uh." She takes a deep breath, *what am I doing*, she berates herself. *Screw it.*

"I lost. *No.* I didn't *lose* — See, my daughter went missing almost seven months ago. She's only thirteen years old, and I was at the library after talking to this kid who told me a story about monster bugs that look human or are infected. I don't know. But when I was at the library, I was researching that sort of thing and then your name came up. Er, number, sorry. Like, not in research, or anything. It just appeared on the computer." Ghini can feel herself wheezing through the litany of words she's just spewed out at record speed.

"Like, on they screen?"

"No. No. Like it was on a slip of paper. Just lying on the keyboard when I got back from getting coffee."

"Where did jou say jou was from?"

"South Dakota. Rapid City."

The silence on the other end is palpable, but Ghini doesn't have to look this time. She knows the woman is still there.

"Yes, I know why jou have —"

The call is interrupted with a flighty beep. A sound Ghini knows too well and forces her into a state of lividness toward herself. It's the sound of not remembering to charge her damn phone. Slowly, she pulls it down to watch as the cell carrier's logo flashes and fades off the screen.

She'd charged her stupid vaporizer rather than her phone. She pulls the blasted addiction device from her pocket and begins to inhale the tasty blueberry nicotine mixture. Though, it doesn't provide the same buzz as normal.

"*Well. Sheeit.*" She exhales a stream of vapor. Damn addiction is going to cost her big time. Cost her a chance to maybe learn the truth.

Learn what happened to Jeannie . . . Involving — bug people?

She sighs and continues to hit the vaporizer, wondering how far would she be willing to go to figure out what happened to Jeannie? She eyes the vaporizer one last time as her stop is called and she gets to her feet neglecting the phone still sitting on her lap. It falls to the floor, face down, and she knows within an instant that the screen is cracked. The anger bubbles up inside her. Frustration and self-loathing breed a beast in her chest.

She grabs the phone and slides it into her back pocket without taking in the damage. She can't bear to let her anger get the best of her right now. Her knuckles are aching with how tightly she's holding the stupid vaporizer to her palm. After getting off to the cold cement sidewalk, she eyes the piece of crap one last time and slams it into the trash.

I'll go as far as it takes to get my little girl back.

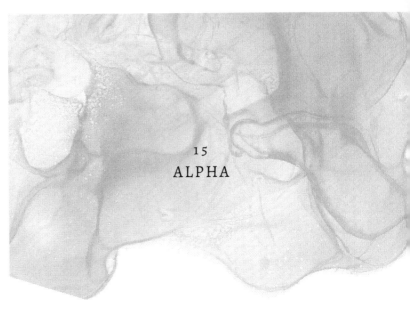

15

ALPHA

"And that makes eight," Mel says to herself.

A grin creeps up a lone dimpled cheek. It emphasizes a face more round and squirrelly than ever before. An aesthetic helped in large part thanks to a set of clippers that she'd used to buzz her hair down to a thick half inch. Now her scalp appears as if it's been matted in a violently red, abnormal strain of grass.

She prepares to usher in their last arrival of the evening. With her eyes flipped, she can make out all the girl's minute details from a distance. This one wears the same look as all the rest. Pale and dazed, yet *joyful* — no that isn't it. She looks like she's on something. They all do. A drug permitting an expression of genuine happiness to blanket their faces.

With her dark lipstick and dark eye shadow, Mel thinks, *this one looks dangerous.* The latter of which forms malevolent points that swoop away from her eyes. As if pointing toward the frame of dark natural curls cropped into a helmet-like bob. It all washes out her already pale skin, nearly concealing the thick silver ring piercing the septum of her nose and the matching collection of silver rings in her ears.

Mel ballparks this one's age around twenty-one, maybe twenty-two. She's definitely on the younger end of this evening's batch.

Like most of the women who arrive, this one will need a change of clothes after her assimilation. She's dressed in a tight crop-top that accentuates her skin-and-bones figure. She leaves little to the imagination, this one. A tiny leather skirt hugs her boney hips. The kind that reminds Mel of bitter little girls with shrill mocking voices.

This must be the one that Kari said she had hypnotized at a "club" — like these podunk mountain towns possessed such a thing. Thankfully, Mel knows that's likely for the best. Big places have big followings and big eyes all around, restaurants, hotels, pubs. Too many stories muddle a disappearance like that.

But, in a small podunk tourist spot like this, everyone's going to make an impact on someone.

It's chilly, this evening, yet Mel doesn't note a single goose-bump atop the girl's bared flesh. She takes this to mean the girl might have a bit of a tolerance for the cold. It's in her blood, an advantage.

Evolution allows many predators to adapt, and Mel takes note of all the evolutionary benefits of her sisters.

As she begins to guide the girl in, she hears the footsteps echo deep within the hallowed walls.

The cave is a maze of tunnels, and Mel has already familiarized herself with much of the layout. Each chamber is so eloquently outlined in a system that resonates with her most basic instincts. She knows the footsteps approaching, and she knows where they're coming from, but more importantly, how much time she has.

She quickly wipes the sweet nectary saliva from her tongue to the tip of a finger and dips it into the girl's mouth as if she were fingering something from a dog's jowls. Though a dog would put up more of a fight. The girl does nothing.

"What are you doing Mel?" Kari asks aloud. Her hands were still flecked with wet and drying mud from her assimilation efforts. "You shouldn't be this close to the entrance."

"*Someone* should be here for our new sister. Don't you agree?" Mel stares down her sister with her sapphire-esc honeycombs. She prefers it this way, but she doesn't like how Queenie carries herself around her when she keeps her eyes this way too long. But she knows it drives Kari mad — and that she enjoys.

But what she enjoys most, is the ability to make out all those tiny details on Kari's face. The tightening of the skin around the petty woman's jaw always brings a sense of triumph to Mel's heart.

"Well. Thank you Mel. That'll be all for now, you should probably go to bed, and get warm. I would have at least hoped you'd get something for our new sister, a coat perhaps on this chilly night. Surely, you could have given her *yours*. Though she won't need it now. Will you Sierra?"

Sierra passes Kari. The trance-like look remains on her face, as she strides directly toward where she needs to go.

Suddenly Queenie is there. Dark rings have formed under her unchanging honeycomb eyes, but she remains her usual bubbly self. "I can't remember the last time I stayed up this late!" She dances toward their sisterhood's final addition of the evening. Without hesitation, she grabs the girl's face and lands a long and heavy kiss that echoes a dramatic *mwhaa* across the cave walls.

"Now that's all this Queenie's got in her for the evening. I'll need you ladies to make sure that our newest sister —"

"Sierra." Mel chimes in, catching the look that Kari gives her. Oh, how it brings Mel such delight to see those tiny micro-movements across Kari's face. Even now, her mouth remains wide open. The *S* of their sister's name still frozen on the tip of her tongue.

"*Sierra*. Such a pretty name my dear. Make sure she's put away properly Kari. She'll be the last to rise tomorrow, and we'll need to make sure that someone's around to show her the ropes in the morning too."

"*It'll-all-be-taken-care-of,*" Kari lets out the flutter of words, with a smug grin. She wasn't going to let that little bald bitch beat her to it this time.

Though, for Mel, it's more effort to bite back the laughter welling up in her sides. She pictures Kari in pigtails, lording herself over the husky girls at recess. Mel contains her glee to a smile.

"Relax my sweet Kari." Queenie yawns. "I think the cold is getting to you. I can feel your tension. Why don't you come to bed with me?" She turns and saunters only a few steps. "*Come.*" The last bit isn't a request, and Kari looks smug, like the brown-noser who's won the teacher's affection.

But Mel knows that the winners are those who don't have the teacher's eyes on them.

"Mel, you can handle our sweet Sierra on your own, yes? You've been watching us this evening?"

"Yes, mother. Consider her in good hands." She smiles wide, and with her short hair looks somewhat like a little boy, but her curvy figure breaks that illusion quickly.

"Thank you. Also, I forgot to say. I don't think many of us could pull off that hair, but you look as beautiful as ever my vibrant daughter." She strides back past Kari and bends to land a kiss atop Mel's fuzzy head.

The pheromones from Queenie are intoxicating, but Mel

has her wits enough to let them be Kari's for the night. At the end of the day, they're nothing more than smells, and what Mel is after is so much stronger.

"Thank you mother." She says with a slight bow to hide the grin she's incapable of concealing. Thankfully, she rises just in time to see that beautiful flicker of jealousy tighten Kari's block jaw.

With the abundance of sweet saliva filling her mouth, Mel couldn't be any happier with herself and how this has all played out.

16

WITCHING HOUR

V rrrrrp - Vrrrrrp - Vrrrrrp -

The clock reads 3:11 AM. *Who's calling at this hour?* Ghini hopes it isn't work. She's been awake most of the night and feels like a zombie. Though, the same goes for the night before. Kept awake by anxiety and amphetamines.

She goes to silence the phone, knowing to keep an eye on the screen to avoid slicing her finger on the fresh cracks. The unfortunate outcome of the bus incident. An anxious dread seeps into every bit of her reality. That crack, that call, and the fact that she hasn't been able to get ahold of that number, all amplify her anxiety. Just as she's about to swipe the call away, three numbers, familiarly arranged, stun her momentarily.

309.

Hastily, Ghini throws aside any caution regarding the cracks.

"Don't hang up." The woman's voice on the other end is different from before. Whoever speaks now sounds younger.

Gone is the Hispanic accent, in favor of a bland midwestern cadence.

"Who is this?" Ghini asks, picking crust from her eyes.

"Please. Just listen. I won't be able to talk long, there's something you have to hear *ASAP*." The woman instructs Ghini to call her Kay. Though in her mind, it's like, *Men In Black*. Just the letter. K.

"Did you know the earliest origination of insect species could possibly date as far back as *480 Million Years?* Do you know what that *means?*" The woman speaks so swiftly that Ghini wouldn't have had a chance to answer if she did know. "It *means* insects likely evolved through, at minimum, *four* of the five major mass extinctions!"

K strikes Ghini as long-winded, and she's not sure she has the patience for the woman's babbling.

"However, it is fairly agreed upon amongst the scientific community that we are currently — *eh, roughly* — ten thousand years into the sixth. The catalyst, of course, being man. Well, not *men*. Although, they kind of *are* the problem for everything. Aren't they?" She snorts a chuckle and continues.

"That is to say, many species have gone extinct at the hands of man. Such is the case with all mass extinction catalysts, life must evolve to survive or perish. Dogs for instance. Becoming domesticated ensures their survival. A symbiotic relationship. Give and take. Well, insects are different. Most people shriek at the sight of the *teency-weenciest* six-legged critter. Imagine *those* people around the eagle-sized dragonflies of the Permian Period! Priceless!"

Ghini has had enough of the woman's rambling. "Ma'am it is 3:30 in the fuckin' mornin', and if you are crank calling me, I swear to God, I will beat the color out ya damn eyes."

"Oh. Yes. Yes. Of course. My apologies." A deep breath rattles the line. "Over time, insects have been astounding examples of Darwinism. No matter what the galaxy has thrown at them — quite literally, I might add — they have *survived*." The inflection resembles that of a proud mother.

"However, man has presented the most current obstacle. Our own evolution, developing civilization, has expedited the destruction of many species. Have you ever heard of the parasitoid wasp? Eh, I'll explain regardless. It's my passion." Another snort. "*Parasitoid* wasps lay their larvae, the *parasite*, in a host. Note the distinction. Sorry, there's the lecturer again." Her piggy laugh echoes once more.

"An adaptation permitting them to spawn offspring on or *in* the body of living organisms. Well, a tale exists among entomologists. Told in hushed tones, more often a campfire story than anything. But I know there is a truth to it.

"The world changed at the dawn of man, but the birth of civilization expedited retroactive evolution. Likely an early parasitoid tried *and failed* to use man as its breeding ground. Many would give up, but species will adapt in different ways to their environment.

"The records of history originate, and we see the birth of the lycanthrope, er uh, werewolf mythos. We see it in Gilgamesh, Ancient Greece, even Nordic mythologies. The hubris of man dictated that a tiny insect couldn't be feared. A wolf though. They themselves were beasts. So, men, and I do mean men, did as they do. They embellished stories, created fear. Combine that with the gate-keeping of knowledge, and you have power.

"These parasitoid creatures hide within the gutters of history, but they're not invisible. What I know to be clear, *women*, exclusively women, are depicted in the earliest records. I believe a connection likely exists to the Amazonians of Greek mythology as well. The similarities of strength, reflexes, and hyper-senses that should be the thing of myth, are startling.

"Not only that but physical deformities too. Body structures mutating over a fortnight, becoming insectoid. Normal eyes developing into *pseudopupils*. Sound *familiar?*"

It does. Alertness courses through Ghini's veins. Memories of the other day in the church echo its dry arid interior across her arms.

"These earliest depictions then abruptly end. I personally believe that had Alexander the Great's Library not burned, we'd have access to a wealth of knowledge about these creatures, alas that isn't possible.

"Now is the portion where I speculate and interject most. I believe they reproduce through the methodology pertaining to most monster mythoi. Not a bite, *but fluids.* Performing like a virus. It would have easily been contained. A precursor to the plagues of old. Not being nearly as deadly, and only victimizing women likely allowed the stories to whither alongside the erosion of history."

Keeping up with K's train of thought is an effort in and amongst itself for Ghini. But she thinks she has an idea where this is going.

"But then something pops up. A *Typhoid Mary.* A *Parasitoid Peggy,* if you will." The snort stifles this time. "Sorry. A Scandinavian woman, asymptomatic to the infection's predominantly deadly prognosis. She somehow *saved* the afflicted women. All of them. Though, that word choice hardly seems appropriate.

"This, I surmise should have been around the fifteenth or sixteenth century. For in the seventeenth, we begin seeing traces of the Haitian zombie mythos, followed shortly thereafter by Eastern European vampire lore. Now, there's no time to get into their re-appearance with the zeitgeist, but we know what man did.

"They fought. They burned. They *culled* until the women all fled . . . or died." A long sigh heaves through the line.

What had started as a lecture, has indeed engrossed Ghini like a terrifying campfire story. The quiet of the darkened living space, washed in the blue glow of the TV adds to the ambiance.

"But they evolved. As Darwin dictated they should. This time returning for the men, whom the parasitoids had only considered to be insufficient hosts, unfit to bear the progeny. However, that's why genealogical memory is such a powerful thing. The parasitoids, alongside their genealogy, gained sentience through the parasitic control of women. Then passed down that genealogical knowledge. So, when they returned, the desire was to develop the males of our species into the image of their own."

Ghini's research had shown her that many male insects were nothing more than single-minded drones.

"The infection withers men. I believe this may have to do with the Y chromosome, but regardless, my investigations have shown they neglect their own needs for that of the master. *The Queen.*" A heavy pause looms over the line, and Ghini fears breaking it might mean bad luck.

K comes back, noticeably more quiet than before. "Like most every insect, these parasitoids can't survive the winter. So, the Queen and her workers move to warmer climates, still, they're instinctual creatures. Meaning they prepare a *foundress* prior to departure. Should she survive, this new Queen hatches come Spring, beginning the cycle anew."

She knows without a shadow of a doubt, where this is going. Despite the doctoral grade lecture she's digesting, Ghini finds her voice. There's one burning question on her mind as the line sits silent once more. "Why are you telling me all of this?"

The palpable quiet endures. She needs to hear K say it.

"*Hello.*" Ghini reiterates, irritation leaking through.

"Yes. I'm here." A biting whisper comes back. "I tell you, because I am *afraid*. The timeline of your daughter's disappearance fits. I *know* a colony could do well in the Black Hills. More than that, these things are intelligent. And they can walk among us. In the daylight. Given our modern-day advances, I fear they have a chance to be more than small colonies. But, more than anything, I fear for *you*. Because I don't want you to end up like —" The line goes silent.

Except, this time Ghini waits several minutes before whispering, "*Like who?*"

The line isn't dead. The call is still active. Yet, K is gone.

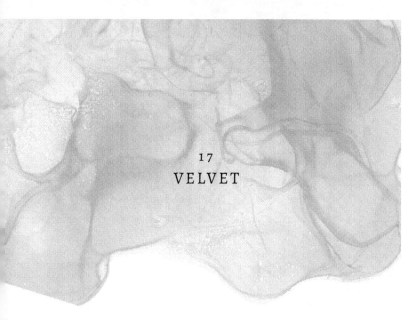

17

VELVET

With the light-footed steps of a ballerina, Mel maneuvers past her sleeping sisters without waking a soul. It's warm this morning, and she enjoys the freedom of the open air at the cave's exit.

The tunnels are becoming cramped. They have more than enough space, but they desperately cling together for warmth, most trying to get as close to Queenie as possible. Thankfully, there are no hatchlings for the first morning in several days. Mel enjoys seeing their numbers grow, epitomizing their budding strength. Still, she has several gripes regarding some sisters, and the way politics is beginning to shape the hive.

Not to mention fucking Kari.

The brown-noser spends more time with Queenie than anyone, but Mel has found her own place. She studies her siblings, strategically spending time with those she sees as fit — the beginnings of a gambit as she has chosen to play Kari's game.

"Hey there Velvet." The nickname has grown on her. It

reminds her of one of her strongest pieces on the board. Sierra. The girl had a strange affinity for studying bugs.

The other day, while *foraging*, Mel had spotted a bright red fuzzy ant crawling across the forest floor. Sierra had instructed her and the others in their little cohort that it was a 'velvet ant.'

'They're actually more closely related to a wasp! Except, the females don't have wings. And they're parasitoids too! They lay their eggs in other insects' nests next to the other eggs! Then their larvae feed off the other larvae! They're crazy. Plus back in Texas, we call 'em 'Cow Killers' on account that they sting so bad the pain'd kill a cow.'

With her fuzzy red hair, the girls had taken to calling Mel, *Velvet*.

"Morning Sierra."

"Whatcha thinkin' about?"

"That name. It suits my new life. I feel —" She'd likely never say this to anyone but Sierra, "I feel like this was who I was meant to be. My *perfect* version."

"You know it's funny, I've thought the exact opposite." Velvet shoots a raised eyebrow. "Well, like, I feel like we should be brainless, mindless zombies, with no personalities. Instead, I feel like me. Just my everyday true self, ever since, ya know . . ." She mimes a sloppy kiss that if Velvet didn't know better could be misconstrued as a dog lapping at the air.

True self? Maybe. Maybe mine had just been dormant. "Hadn't really thought about it like that."

"Like, we all just wake up, and we're not all that different. Well ya know, besides the whole, super strength, 1990's model bodies, freaky eyes, and, of course, the *hunger*. Other than *that*, we're basically still the same."

Sierra often brings a smile to Velvet's face. It's not just her

Texas twang, she's genuinely funny. Still, Velvet finds herself ruminating.

Before this, I was a nobody. Wandering through nowheresville, destined to do the same nothing that my mother did. Now though, I'm free.

Velvet flips into her hive eyes. She feels the energy of the sun's warmth coarse through her. Nourishing her. "Yeah. But what girl doesn't love super strength?" They both laugh.

"Okay. So, what's the plan today? Queenie says we need to get more food for the mouths, not more mouths."

"Oh, she's up?" Velvet immediately begins walking.

Sierra catches up quickly with her long strides. "Sure she is. But she's inventorying the new sisters. Re-educating them on the rules again."

"Kari right at her side?" Sierra nods an affirmative. "Perfect. She's smothering Queenie. A Queen doesn't need a babysitter. She needs workers."

"I mean in a wasp colony, the Queen does often have a sort of support system, so she can just keep pumping out little larvae."

"What an existence. Luckily our Queen doesn't have to do that bit. We just bring them to her and she's got to give them her *likkle* kiss, as she'd say."

Sierra's elbow finds the top of Velvet's ribcage, before adding, "and she doesn't even have to do that bit anymore, does she?"

Sometimes Sierra's laugh gets a bit nasally, and it assaults Velvet's ears like nails on a chalkboard, but her sister is such a wealth of knowledge that Velvet does her best to put up with it.

IT ISN'T long before they reach their secluded watering hole. Both women maneuver over stones and roots to the edge of a ridge overlooking a pristine pond below.

With a twirl, Velvet drops and grabs the lip of the rock at the last second. As she hangs, she sees the ledge, swings her hips, arcing her momentum, and releases on a perfect trajectory for the landing. A quick shimmy is all that's left. Sierra swiftly lands at her side, and the pair are wedged through the crevice that leads to their hidden cave.

Switching to their hive eyes, the two women can let in as much light as possible. All the cracks in the cave's ceiling allow for brittle razors of light to sneak through. The place is dim. Sounds echo throughout without any idea of their origin. Whether from the peaks above or the water below. It lacks the tunnel system of Queenie's hive, but also the accouterments. They haven't put up any lights and what they do have they keep at the back of the short damp walk. There they have a stash of clothes, blankets, and a lone cooler that had been carefully curated.

"It's amazing how much stuff Queenie just has lying around, and how easy it is to pilfer." Sierra says.

"Well, if *we* operate as you say, then it wasn't her that would have amassed it all. Who knows how many Queens have made colonies there, over time. I mean some of these coats and gloves look *ancient*." They do. Highlighter colors, overly puffy, and patchworks of patterns that have long since gone out of style.

As they hoist some of their haul, Sierra adds, "Do you ever notice, no matter what, Queenie's eyes never change from hive eyes? Do you think it hurts? My eyes hurt the longer I go."

"I doubt it hurts, maybe they're just stuck that way. I mean she could be 100 years old for all we know, and is just used to it. But, I mean, even I have gotten better, and I hatched being able to hold hive eyes for hours when others were minutes."

As Velvet gets the fire going, the pair sit on the ground staring up at the four muddy chrysalises.

"Do you really think she could be 100 years old?" Sierra asks swirling a stick in the heart of the flames.

"Could be. Though, as you said, she'd have to have survived winter somehow." The only sound in the tiny alcove comes from the crackling wood beneath the flames.

"It won't even take winter." Sierra's gaze falls to the body lying in the corner.

"True."

Queenie told them to fear the cold. Sierra on the other hand taught Velvet that many insects began dying if the temperature dropped below fifty. So, while everyone played it safe, the pair had run an experiment, proving a hypothesis from Sierra that "we're smarter than insects, and we should survive the cold and the winter." This also felt like confirmation of Velvet's original deduction about Sierra herself. She had retained a genetic tolerance to the cold.

Though, what experiment was complete without a control? Their guinea pig's death was chalked up as an unfortunate accident. A newbie that many blamed Kari for, saying she had not explained the rules properly. So, Velvet used that moment to have Sierra educate the hive on what the pair already knew.

Velvet laughs and Sierra's eyes drift back to her. A malicious excitement lies beneath her blotchy eyeliner.

Everything is going to plan.

Velvet has enjoyed watching the girl thrive underneath her. She took direction best from Velvet, and no one knew more about bugs than her, a rather handy trait.

Suddenly, one of the chrysalises begins to crack. Sierra

prepares a warm seat, while Velvet drags the corpse like a child with their blanket. As their sister begins to emerge, Velvet takes a bite from the calf muscle. She savors the sweet decaying flavor as the natural ichor drains down the sides of her lips. Her mouth naturally produces the delicious nectar in response. Her trump card. Something only she and Queenie are capable of, so far.

She grabs the hatchling's slender jaw and forces her tongue into the woman's mouth, sliding the sweet nectar along the surface. She then grabs Sierra and gives her a taste as well.

Both women look on with dulled eyes and warm smiles. Their hive eyes flutter out, and Velvet feels that first maternal pang of love seeing the way the two sets gaze at her.

"Okay Sierra, get her fed, our precious —"

"Shadezrhia."

"Right. I'm going with Dezi." Velvet adds. "Now, I'll be back in a second, I'm going to check on our guest."

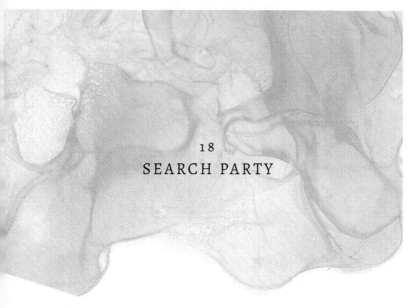

18

SEARCH PARTY

"Found something!" Samuel hollers. The girl's parents move with a lack of urgency. The same can't be said for Detective Dakota Johnson.

It's a cell phone, an older model by the looks of it. The screen's cracked — badly. Taking the phone with his gloved fingers, Dak asks the parents if it belongs to their daughter.

Samuel had been walking through a wilderness campsite when he'd noticed what appeared to be signs of a struggle. Faint drag lines had outlived the elements and led off into the woods. On the edge of the site, he'd spotted the metallic shine.

The girl's father, who's as Texas as can be, strides up in his ornate burnt-orange cowboy boots, longhorn belt buckle, and hat to match. "I dunno. Could be." He stares intently.

The girl's mother is dressed like she's never been out in nature before. Her 'hiking' attire still has creases in it, having likely been recently purchased under the guise that she was planning to climb Everest.

"No-sir-ee-Bob, she'd never be caught dead with an old junker like that. Sierra always had to have the newest and best.

I made sure of it! Gosh, she was such a sweet angel. Why'd that horrid boy have to convince her to come to this backwater town? Ronnie, you never should have let her go on that trip!"

She begins to sob crocodile tears. Neither Samuel nor Dak are movie buffs, but both sure as hell know the woman is as bad of an actor as they come. She bickers with her husband in a manner unfit for the multitude of law enforcement agents and volunteers in present company. The drama of their squabble pales in comparison to where both men's minds have gone.

Dak looks how Samuel feels, annoyed and tired. But he does his job and bags the phone, sensing in his gut, the same thing that Samuel is thinking — that it might very well prove useful to a different open case.

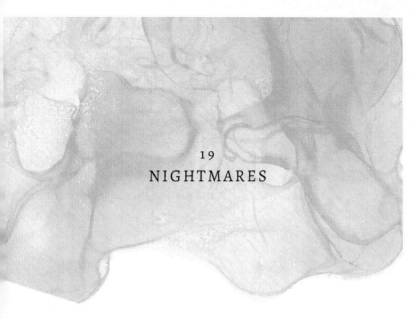

19

NIGHTMARES

Ghini had kept K's call active for hours, but she never heard another word or sound.

She finally gave up when another call came through. It'd been Samuel.

A girl from Texas, on a spring break trip with her boyfriend went missing in the hills. He'd asked if she wanted to join the search party. She'd declined knowing she'd struggle right alongside those poor parents.

It's been several days since that ominous call from K. She's tried calling back each morning around that same 3:30 hour, but the phone has either died or been switched off. To Ghini, it's like she'd been thrown a lifeline, only to have it ripped away before she could grasp it.

The days since, have been taxing. When Bernie had told her that she should just have the funeral and move on, she was angry. She was in denial. But now, she lives with a darker prospect.

Was Jeannie a monster? An abomination?

She'd rejected a lone person saying that to her. But as time passed, acceptance tried to worm its way into her heart. It arrived faster when a second person had chimed in with the same nightmarish horrors...

Since K's call, Ghini hasn't had any real sleep. She'd gone so far as to work a double yesterday to keep herself busy. The two days prior, she'd come in early and stayed late. Now she just can't do it. She can't bring herself to go in at all.

She's planning to call in sick tonight. Instead, committed to festering in the darkness of her apartment. Letting the idea of a dark reality gnaw away at her soul from the lightless void she refuses to leave. A place where her Jeannie was...

She's hardly eaten, the Adderall helps with the hunger pains, but she feels jittery and flighty and knows that sleep is in desperate need.

Then there are — *the dreams.*

The ones that eek their way in after she's accidentally nodded off. Her baby walks in as if nothing's happened — with those pseudopupil eyes. Then it gets worse. Pincers burrow out from her cheeks and antennae burst from the crown of curls on her head. It's too much. Sometimes Jeannie pleads —

"*Help.*" It's a scratchy wine.

Occasionally it's a desperate, "*Save me momma.*"

Other times she hears, "*Please momma, I don't want to live like this.*" That's the one that haunts her.

Those dreams scare her more than the other ones — where Jeannie is nothing more than Ghini's worst fears.

Her hands have morphed into stilleto-esc claws that rip into Ghini's flesh. A frightening strength nails her to the floor. Then the pincers explode from Jeannie's cheeks, dripping with ichor and a slimy mucus. Pinned beneath that formidable strength, Ghini watches on as what was once her little girl, now a monster, eviscerates her very being. She wakes from those dreams screaming and in a sweat. Her skin tingles in those places she'd been mauled.

She'd had to stop going to the library after nodding off into one of those dreams in particular. Not that it mattered. She was too spent to be embarrassed and too defeated to hope another note might finally appear.

No more notes had come. There was no sign of the barista, and her searches for any information about the creatures were fruitless. No one seemed to know the missing barista either. It was as if she'd never actually existed.

Then there'd been all the news stories about the little emo white girl who went missing. It was every headline this week, and Ghini felt like she was reliving a nightmare worse than anything she'd dreamt because she couldn't escape this one. She wanted no part in helping with the search efforts, predominately out of fear of what they might find.

Even when the voices in her head told her she was a bad mother and a hypocrite for not doing so.

Why did she ever let Jeannie go on that damn field trip?

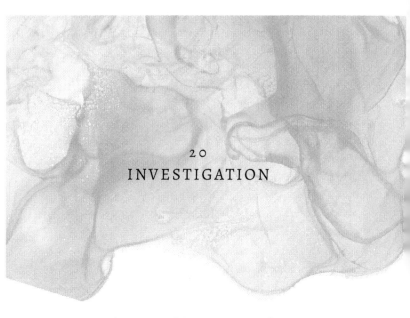

2 0

INVESTIGATION

ho are you, Morgan Humes?" Detective Dakota Johnson whispers to himself.

Dak has been sitting at his desk since, well, it had been dark out. Now the morning is obtusely present. The sun showers the bullpen floor in a golden glow. It's too nice a morning. Grey skies and cracking thunder would better suit his mood.

He's had no luck tracking down the owner of the phone Clemens had found. Unfortunately, the name Morgan Humes produces a lot of results — and until he gets his warrant, he's stuck with a long list.

After dusting for prints and sending those off, Dak got the thing on a charger. As soon as it could flicker back to life, he had it hooked up to a desktop. That way he won't need to risk slicing open a finger on the cracked screen. Mirroring the device, he checks for missed calls, voicemails, or texts across the top ticker.

Empty.

Next, he'd descended into the man's camera roll. Checking

the geo-tags might help him get an idea of Humes' last move-ments before he went dark. Maybe even trace back to a home address. Except, the guy's camera roll is a ghost town save for a handful of photos of the Hills around the campsite. Not a single useable piece of info. No selfie, or group photo, not a single thing that can help Dak ID Humes or his counterparts.

With that dead end, he heads back to Humes' call and text logs. The man only has a handful of names in his phone, and it appears he'd have been lucky to send more than five texts in a given week. Someone named Brandon, no last name, is Humes' most frequent contact. They share a couple group threads. The smaller and more active of the two is a wealth of information and is likely where Dak should have started.

It explicitly details a camping trip with not only this Bran-don, but also a Landon, and Tristan as well. No last names for any of them.

He scribbles down, *old friends? Landon, Brandon, Tristan, and Morgan.*

He pictures a boyband and can't help but chuckle.

Though it does start to give him a profile. Adding together the sparse contacts, lack of photos, the older model of smart-phone, and Dak has a picture of a man likely born before 1985. He's single, no kids or pets, and either self-employed or in a profession where he isn't missed. It wouldn't shorten his list by much, but it paints a picture of a good victim.

Dak then roped in a uniformed officer, asking her to reach out to the other numbers in the group text. Although, he's still disappointed when she strolls back within minutes carrying the news he'd expected. All three went straight to voicemail.

Dak still hasn't gotten his warrant for the cellphone records, and the fingerprints won't be back any time soon, so he tries his luck at combing the net. Only to be hit with the realization that they lack enough information to narrow the list further. Then there's Humes' recent search history. For the most part, it's nothing but camping-related questions, and a few queries regarding bugs, bears, and wolves.

Nah it's the big horns to watch out for here.

Otherwise, the phone is desolate. Not even an email account or some games.

"How's it going old man?" Detective Jontay Legends saunters off the elevator with the pride of youth.

"Mornin' Legends." Then an idea hits him. "Wait. Legends, you're a child of the '90s. Tell me, aint this weird to see a guy with a blank phone?"

Legends slides his way across the linoleum with a fervor to see the mysterious device. The young detective, with his hightop fade, and natural good looks, nods as if to ask for permission to grasp the mouse. Of course Johnson wants to know what the kid can find, so he slides it a generous centimeter — a show of, *'c'mon then, get to it.'*

The kid's eyes fixate on the monitor. "Woah. This is wild, man. I can't even recall the last time I seen somebody without even Facebook, ya know? Shit, guy doesn't even have *Candy Crush* or *Angry Birds*. Dude's either a pedo or a spook. Guessing nothing from fingerprints?"

"Not yet. Hard to expedite prints for a missing adult male with no signs of foul play. We only got his name from the phone itself. Otherwise, the digital fingerprint is about as non-existent as I've ever seen. So, unless you can dig something up, looks like we're on hold until we get prints back or a warrant."

"Okay, okay, okay. Do we even know it's a guy? Morgan's a pretty gender-neutral name. What are *these* names?" He points to Brandon, Landon, and Tristan scrawled on a piece of yellow legal paper.

"Should be his *last seen with*. Good ole boys trip."

"Hmmm. So Tristan's kinda like Morgan here. We could be looking at a group of four guys or a pair of couples? We have no signs of any of these guys?"

"Nope. All I've got is the phone and the fact that a fire was in that pit sometime in the last two to three weeks, give or take."

"Okay, okay, okay . . . What's more likely here? Our recluse is out there alone or that he's with others?"

Dak's been asking himself that question for hours, and it frustrates him just thinking that the kid doesn't even realize that.

"You've probably been asking that for hours now." *Or maybe he does.* "Okay, okay, okay. Then what questions are left? What can Legends do for ya?" He scans the phone physically, before going back to the monitor where he peruses the app screen.

"Wait! Wait! Wait, a second! What's this?" Dak perks up at the kid's enthusiasm. "This app here. The eye!"

"I don't know."

"See here. It ain't a system default. Let's see . . . okay. Okay. Oh-kay!"

"*Okay, what?*"

"It's a video recording app with some nifty features. Records while the screen is off, and will keep recording until low battery hits. Then will stop itself and save the recording."

"Explain it to me. Why would anyone have that? Seems sketchy."

"Guy could be a creep *fersure.* Or a videographer. Maybe both? If it's the latter it'd be good for collecting b-roll footage or time-lapses while still conserving battery. Maybe he's a P.I.?"

"Is there anything there?"

"Ohhh, you betcha! Cloud backup enabled! Let's! Go! Now

let me in, you shy little bastard. Would you look at that! Eleven days ago. Recording backed up."

"Wait. Legends . . ."

"Hold on. I know it's not identical. But there's overlap with the timeline for the Kalisch disappearance, yeah?" The young man's face twinkles like only a child's on Christmas can. "Do you think?"

Dak's following. "I ain't saying till we got more to go on. What's the date exactly?"

They get that time frame written down and pass it off to the same uni as earlier. This time, there's a glimmer of hope she'll come back with something that can shorten their Morgan Humes list.

"Aren't they far apart, like geographically?" Legends wonders aloud. "Kalisch went missing *in* Deadwood. This phone was found where?"

"Maybe an hour away. Depending on weather and tourist season." He can't rule out the connection, but something else nags him more. "This is a huge leap from anything the department'd be willing to say, but if this is foul play, these were four grown humans, likely men. Either we're dealing with a terrifying single unsub . . . or *multiple*."

"Shit — that'd be a career maker Dak!"

It would be. But the kid's still young, he doesn't see the other side. What it'd mean for all sorts of missing persons cases stretching back years. And how many more are likely to come.

"So, we're going to play this thing right?"

Dak lets out a heavy exhale before pulling the mouse back.

At first, it's just footage of the ground. Close up, though it is moving. It looks like the phone's being slid an inch or so over the dirt. Dak's mind goes toward someone crawling on their elbows, the phone in their hand. There is some audio, but it's muffled, likely confirming his theory.

"Fuck." Legends sighs under his breath.

Dak thinks he's heard it too. Through the gagged microphone, both men hear what sounds like cries of violent pain. The kind most people only hear on TV. In real life, detectives are only ever involved long after the screams end. A noticeable shiver marches down each man's spine.

Suddenly, the videographer is trying to stand up. The phone then goes flying through the air and tumbles into the brush where Clemens had found it.

A significant *thud* makes each man think that the videographer hit the ground. But there are at least two distinct thuds, maybe three.

Could he have been tackled?

There's no way of telling what the sounds were, but with the mic clear, they can hear voices approach. They're a bit stifled, but there's a woman's voice clear as day.

"I think we need to put him down, sweet Kari."

Dak is quick to make note of the pronunciation.

Car-Ee.

Only a second later, a sickening *crunch* gives way to a wet *squelch*. The two men sit in silence staring at the motionless image of grass and forest debris.

"Thank you, my dear. Let's grab one of the tents and roll them up in it. Then grab another and roll up their belongings."

There's some more audio, but it's garbled and distant. They might be able to have forensics clean it up, but for now, only a few things seem clear.

A woman named *Car-Ee*, and a female accomplice were present.

The two women stole *all* the men's belongings, considering there wasn't a single trace of the men's stay at the campsite.

And most importantly, they need to get back out there, as this has officially become a homicide investigation.

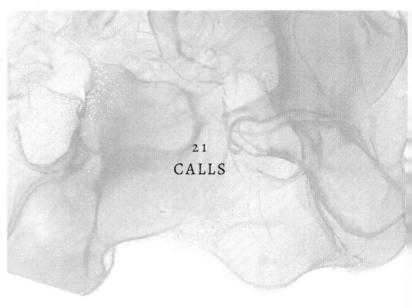

2 1
CALLS

Ghini can't believe he's calling her, but she's glad to hear another human's voice.

"Ya know I hate callin'."

"I know Samuel."

"Then know what I'm telling ya, well, it's important." He pauses, giving her a moment to settle. "I found something while looking for that Texas girl."

Ghini's heart skips a beat. What could he have found? What could be so important that Samuel Clemens would make a phone call?

But not important enough for the police to call . . .

"A cellphone. It weren't the girl's, but Jeannie's phone were never found?"

She shakes her head before realizing he can't see her. "No. No, it wasn't."

"Could be hers. Can't remember anything bout it, but if it's neither girl's . . ." He trails off. Letting her finish the idea before adding, "I'm just sayin', might be time to open yer mind to the idea of why people go missing in The Hills."

A part of her brain screams. Tell him off for calling her close-minded, for thinking she hasn't been doing her own work.

But, that voice, that version of herself feels disingenuous. That's an archaic version that could live in blind ignorance, self-medicating on hope, and ultimately cracking under the weight of her deep emotions — she's pretty sure she'll never be that fragile woman again. And the more she feels herself distancing from that life of denial, the more Ghini realizes she has the drive in her to never be that erratic close-minded woman ever again.

"What'd they find on it?" She asks. Knowing it's not exactly the warm response she meant, but Ghini needs to know.

"I don't know. Just thought you should."

The dead air between them alerts Ghini that Samuel is about to hang up — and it's now or never for her to check her pride. Samuel is someone she needs in her life. "Wait! Samuel. I *might* be a little more *trusting* than you think."

The words sit between them, but she's becoming an expert at knowing the line is still open. "Go on."

"Yeah. See, I went to the library. I've *been* going to the library. Like every day since we saw Bernie. I was being *watched*, though. Before you ask, I don't know who. It was the first day. I got a coffee and came back to a slip of paper with a phone number. I called it late that evening and a Hispanic woman picked up, but my phone died." A tinge of embarrassment leaks into her words.

Why does she never charge her damn phone?

"Then a different woman calls me back, and I know she's different because she's got no accent. I checked the area code, says she's from Illinois, at least the number she called off was. I double-checked too, it's the same number from the slip.

"Anyway, I'm listening to this lady, and understand it's like three in the mornin' several days later. But she's goin' on-n'-on about how there's these monsters that are evolved from insects, but they're the source of like Vampires, Zombies, and Werewolf stories, or whatever.

"So, she prattles on, until, in mid-sentence, she's just gone. Not a fuckin' sound. Just cut off talking. Here's the thing, though. The call never dropped and neither of us hung up. That is until you called me, however many hours later that was.

"I don't know *what's* going on Samuel. I just know I am much more open to the idea of monsters than I thought I was. And your nephew doesn't sound so crazy anymore."

Samuel's letting it all digest. He takes his time.

"And I owe him an apology." She knows that's the ticket to breaking Samuel's silence, but she also knows it's the truth.

"Okay. I'll hold ya to that."

"Wouldn't have it any other way." She feels a smile sneak the corners of her tightlipped mouth upward. It's a nice reminder that she still has Samuel in her life.

"Okay. Next actions?"

Now does not seem like the time for patience. "I don't know! I've looked at so much and — and — " Ghini decides not to tell Samuel about the nightmares, and her struggles.

"I may have an idea then."

"*What?*"

"May know a guy. Done some work together round the reservations a time or two. There've been whispers over the years. I'll reach out. But, you need to figure out what Johnson found on that phone. Get all ya can."

"Then what?"

"Then to the reservation, but I strongly suspect we need that information from Johnson."

"But how'll that help? You hoping to see Bigfoot on camera?"

"Not necessarily."

"Then *what?*"

"Ain't sure. Just have a little *trust.*"

That conversation in Samuel's truck, parked on the side of the highway rockets back to the forefront of Ghini's memory. "Okay. I trust you. I'll call Dak right after this."

"Good. And write down as much as you can remember from that call with the woman."

"You got it."

The air seems to grow stale between them as it's exposed to things left unsaid. But neither can quite bring themselves to say what's next on their minds. A crackle sneaks through the line and panic grips Ghini's chest. She can't let him hang up yet.

"Stay safe, Samuel. I'm *scared.*" It comes out childlike, almost a whisper.

She knows he's still there, but she's worried the old man might not have heard her, or that she just gave him grounds not to work with her.

"I think we all are. Now you do the same Miss Ghini. Stay safe."

AN HOUR HAS GONE BY, and Ghini hasn't found it in her to call Dakota yet. Her reality is on its last leg, and the vulnerability she feels grasping at straws of normalcy is a thing she refuses to let him see.

The merlot has been helping. She'd started with whiskey, but decided to treat herself. The bottle was meant for a special occasion, one that likely would never come now. The acceptance of that fact outweighs her grief, leading to some semblance of serenity — though the half-empty bottle of wine likely plays a role as well. She knows if she doesn't call sooner or later, she'll have gone too far over the edge.

There's a bit of blue powder on her table — ground-up Adderall. She licks the tip of her finger, presses it to the blue dust, and proceeds to line her gums with the sweet yet chemical flavor. The rush isn't far behind. She feels a bit more clear, even if it's just a false, chemically-induced composure.

She stares at his number one last time, clicks the green button, and takes a deep breath.

He answers quickly, "Hello. Ghini?"

"Dakota."

"*Yes?* What's going on here Ghini, is everything okay?" He sounds more stressed than worried.

She wants to keep her cool. To do so she needs to dive in. "Dakota. I hear through the grapevine you may have a new lead in the case of a *missing* girl?"

There's an emptiness in the silence between them.

"Dakota?"

"How'd you hear about that Ghini? *Clemens?*"

"Does it really matter? Mothers have ways. Is it about Jeannie?" She hears the melancholy in her voice, and if he does too, it might do her a favor.

"Listen, it's not related to her case. At least—" It sounds like he's leaning towards being the cop, not the friend. But before Ghini can figure a way to coax him, he gently says, "At least, I don't *think* it is."

"What's that s'posed to mean!" The words are off her tongue before she realizes it. "Dakota, you can't say shit like that! Tell me, what's happened?" Her voice is loud and her chest is hot. This is real. She's lost sight of keeping cool and doesn't care. All she needs are answers. Nothing more than those, and she doesn't have time for their history to get involved. *"Dakota!"*

"Fine, fine." An audible sigh speckles the space between them. "It's possible there could be a group of women out in the Hills, and they could be dangerous. Please, I know I don't deserve anything from you, but I could probably get away with saying I don't owe you shit either . . . So, just keep this between us. Please."

Ghini isn't sure what to say. She's also unsure how she ended up on her knees with the phone on the floor. A tear falls onto the screen, brightening it.

Dakota Bear <3

"Ghini?"

"Sorry. I, I dropped my phone. But I heard you." She chokes back the tears and uses her strength to hide them. "Is that *really* all you know?"

"Okay, I *know* they're violent." He sighs into the receiver. "One man is dead, likely four. We've gotten names, and contacts and no one's heard from them in two weeks."

She should warn him. He needs to know the rest, but Samuel's words from that day echo in her mind. *He needs proof.* That's something she doesn't have. All she has is trust, and she's not sure she deserves that from Dakota.

"Please for the sake of all these girls, you've got to solve this one. Please Dakota. No matter what the evidence says, please do whatever it takes. No more mothers should go through this."

"Okay. I'll do everything in my power. You have my word."

"Thank you. Good night Dakota." *Bear.*

She hangs up and falls to her side, curled around the phone. Her eyes lock on the call-ended screen. She remains there long past when the screen has gone dark.

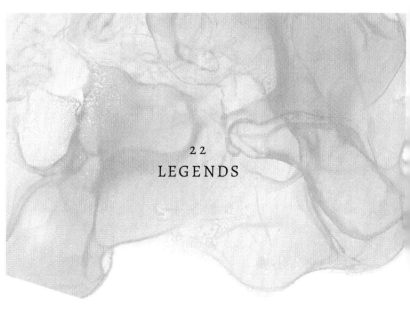

22
LEGENDS

"I'll take a Uni out there with me. You go home and get some rest." Detective Jontay Legends knows Dak will fight him on this, but he also knows the man is going on 16 hours of work, and that won't do the case any good, let alone Dak himself.

Luckily, Officers Bradley and Tomlinson volunteer to go out with Legends. Dak's reassurance comes from the fact that Bradley'd been helping them throughout the morning, and she wasn't just up to speed, she's an all-star. Well on her way to making detective.

Then there's her partner — Tomlinson. On the other hand . . . he's a bit slow, but ultimately a good kid, and a morally sound cop.

With a reservation or two, Dak relents and lets the trio take over the scene for the afternoon.

Technically, it isn't even Rapid City PD jurisdiction, but the County and Staties borrow from the RCPD nearly every other case these days. With everything going on, the different departments have had to work in tandem to cover the oddly tomahawk-shaped Pennington County boundary.

Unfortunately, a flurry of public lawsuits has sprung up recently, forcing the resignation of Sheriff Paolini. With diminished manpower and leadership, it was easy for the Sherriff's office to seek assistance from the RCPD. And the Feds, well, they don't have the strongest presence as of late, and would only tag in if a body was found. They weren't even helping with the Kalisch case, nitpicking that she had *reportedly* gone missing in Deadwood, not the National Forest.

Even though they have Bradley, who'd been on the initial search of the area, it takes thirty minutes to get from the car to the campsite.

They start out attempting to secure the area, though there isn't much the three of them can do other than cordon off the patch of dirt with crime scene tape. They'll need forensics back out here as well, but they aren't available until morning. Bradley mentioned to Legends that she'd pled with the captain to intervene. Unfortunately, forensics are as understaffed as any unit. Not to mention, they had already been dispatched to assist on a DOA scene near The Badlands.

So, here they are, in the warm glow of a cloudless mid-afternoon sky. The task at hand requires an obscene amount of tape before they split up. Bradley takes the perimeter, working her way through the wooded trails. Meanwhile, Legends and Tomlinson work the site. There's something inherently out of place about the husky Tomlinson wandering through the middle of the woods sporting his baggy police blues.

"You found anything yet Tommy?" A nickname. Legends can't recall the man's first name. He's never spent much time with the officer. But he knows a bit about him.

Tomlinson's young, even younger than Legends himself.

Coincidentally, they'd grown up down the street from one another — though, it was a *long* street. Couple that with him being Bradley's partner, and he feels a twinge of obligation to help the kid out.

"Bout as much as you'd expect to see, sir."

Sir. That was new. Legends was used to being, *hey kid.* He much preferred the ring of *Sir.*

"Okay. Keep looking. Call out any signs of blood, struggle, footprints, you name it. Shit, even some garbage, pipe up."

"Uh sir, there's footprints everywhere. How the hell can I tell if it's a suspect's or mine?"

Legends is well aware the kid has a reputation for not being the sharpest tack. Even so, seeing it in action humors him. "Tommy, do you recall why I made you put those rubber bands on your boots?"

"Uhh."

"Uhhhhh."

Whoops. Not exactly good leadership. Get it together, man.

"It's an old fr'ensics trick. No booties? Strap rubber bands around your shoes. So you can differentiate."

"Oh, I don't think they ever taught us that." He looks down, embarrassment burning his pudgy cheeks for having forgotten the bright pink and green rubber bands wrapped around his boots.

"Course they didn't, cuz we should be wearing booties. But I read this in a detective novel, and turns out it works. So I always keep a handful in my coat pocket." He pads the outside of his chest, trying to sound light-hearted.

"Right. Okay."

Damn.

Legends knows not to be so hard on the unis and hates that sometimes it leaches out of him. See, Legends was lucky. He lept through that phase quicker than the average detective.

But, he had *earned* his badge too. He just may have had some help.

People say it all the time. *It helps to know people.* The only thing is, Jontay Legends knows it's even better when people *know you.* As the pride of Rapid City and three-year starting quarterback at South Dakota State — with three consecutive National Titles — he was a household name to this day, all these years later.

But all Legends had ever wanted to be was a detective. It helped that he was good at his job.

Something on the ground catches his eye with the briefest of glints. Normally, it would probably get missed — clearly, it had been. But Legends had just seen his own filling the other week at the dentist. He throws on the gloves and picks not only the dental filling up, but nearby is the tooth it'd come from.

This tooth is rotting and decaying around the empty socket where the filling had been. It seems to be an older filling too. He notes it's not the frequented tooth-colored composite he'd been offered. It's a brownish metal that may have once been silver or gold but has aged. It appears as neglected as the tooth that it had called home.

"How long have *you* been out here?" He whispers to the tooth.

Somehow Tomlinson hears enough to ask a ditzy, *what?* Legends ushers him over, revealing the now bagged tooth and filling.

"Dang. You think this could be from a fight?"

"Ya know, I want it to be. But, can't say. That's a fr'ensics call."

"I think it's *for*-ensics, sir."

"That's what I said, *fr'ensics.*"

"Sir, I don't wanna be disrespectful to a superior, but you

are sorely mispronouncing that word." Tommy's giving him a bit of the business, but Legends appreciates it. Just one of the guys, and it makes him feel better about earlier.

"Noted. But *hey*, if I say *fr'ensics*, then I say *fr'ensics*." He says playfully.

"The thing is, your pronunciation is just annoying for everyone. Hi. I speak for everyone." The voice is a woman's, *maybe a girl's?* But it certainly isn't Officer Bradley's.

The girl appears from the woods, and her figure is eye-catching. The type of waist and hips that Legends eyes naturally trace. She has a bright scarlet buzzcut spread across a wide scalp. She doesn't wear any makeup either. But the more she stares at them with tantalizing bright blue eyes, the more Legends realizes she doesn't need to. Her eyes are stunning. She has a cute button nose, and the kind of cheeks that naturally hold a little color. She almost appears to be blushing.

"What're you doing out here all alone?" Tomlinson asks.

"Oh, I'm not alone. I have a couple friends with me. Maybe you know them?"

There's a rustling behind Legends and Tomlinson. Both men spin on their heels, attempting to not be caught by surprise. Even if it means leaving the redhead unattended behind them.

As if on cue, Officer Bradley appears, trailed closely by another young woman. She has curly black hair, and it takes Legends a second to recognize her. She looks different from the photos at the precinct. She's ditched her emo girl look in favor of the typical white girl hiking aesthetic — yoga pants, puffy vest, and long pastel-colored sleeves.

"I'd say you shouldn't stare Detective, as it is impolite, but you know us Texas girls love a quarterback." She sends Legends a flirtatious wink.

"You're Sierra Kalisch." Despite the lack of a threat, instinct has placed his hand on his service weapon.

"Last I checked, *handsome.*" She says with a devilish smile and another wink. This one seems off. Like her eye just —

"Bradley! You did it! Damn you're good!" Tomlinson cries walking over to his partner, hand extended in the air for a high five.

"*Now,* Detective . . ." Legends jumps at the sound of the voice right behind him. "I'm going to need your help here, and so will my friend Sierra."

He hadn't heard a single footstep, and a chasm of dread erupts in the depths of Legends' gut. A feeling akin to going in for the two-minute drill when the other team's just taken a two-score lead in the fourth.

"See —" the scarlet-haired girl is practically whispering in his ear. "I need you to do something for me."

He takes his eyes off Sierra and looks back to the redhead - - his service weapon drawn.

———

"How do you know this is going to work, Velvet?" Sierra asks as they finish up their meal.

"I just do. Kinda like instinct."

"But Queenie said no men yet."

"That's fine. He's not Queenie's, he's mine."

"I can't believe you can control them too. This changes everything."

"Well, I think your intuition may have been right all along, we were just missing some information. Maybe it's because I was younger when I was assimilated. Or maybe because I'm an earlier generation. Maybe it's genetics? Who knows? But my instincts sure seem to think that I can do anything Queenie can."

"Life is so much more fun with you in it, Velvet!" Sierra flashes a wide, overly zealous grin before adding, "So what's the plan? How much longer do you think until he gets back?"

"I haven't decided, but I'm confident he'll be back before nightfall, and I'll want to put him through the assimilation just to see how much control we can get."

"I hope he does. I hate the cold, even if it doesn't do much to me." She lets out that nasally laugh that claws at Velvet's ears. Though, she is learning to tolerate it. "Do we take *this* back to feed the newborns?"

Velvet wipes her mouth. She'll need to start carrying a change of clothes. "Why not? We can even make our dear friend Legends carry what's left."

"And if he's not back in time?"

"We're more than capable of getting the scraps back. Plus, we've gotten what we wanted." She plays with the badge in her hand.

"True." Sierra wipes her mouth clean as well. They are going to need to start wearing more black and red at this rate, she happily thinks.

"Legends, ya baby-faced genius, what'd you find out there?" Dak feels much more like himself this evening. He needed the rest and appreciated the young detective covering the case for him. *"Legends?"*

The kid's sat at his desk, not really moving or doing anything. He's just staring at his computer monitor. So, Dak goes over and puts a hand on the young man's shoulder. He doesn't startle. He just turns his head and looks upward, meeting Dak's eyes with a vacant expression.

"Hi, Detective Johnson. How are you?"

"I'm good. You alright? You seem off."

"Must be tired. It's been a long one."

"Been there. How bout the scene? You or the Unis find anything?"

Legends is silent. His eyes flutter briefly behind closed eyelids, then open back to that empty stare. "There was a filling." He grins and seems to settle back into his normal self. "Yeah, we found this tooth filling, and it's gotta belong to someone who was there with Humes. I'm sure of it. I'm just a little nervous that it could be planted."

"*Planted?* I think you've been reading too many of those detective novels Legends."

"No sir, hear me out. So, this is a dirt patch in the woods. Can't be vacuumed or bleached or anything. Yet there's no blood. There's no sign of a struggle. There's just this filling and a cellphone.

"So, I ask what's more plausible here? Our missing person or persons were attacked in a dirt opening that the attackers manage to clean up with an immaculate level of cleaning skills, yet somehow neglect a filling and a cellphone? Or that they didn't go missing from that campsite? Instead — presuming they were attacked at all — the perpetrators decided to throw us off the scent of the real crime scene by planting this evidence for us to find. I mean, you said it yourself that the photo geotags are close but not exactly on top of the site, and the video doesn't even have a tag, I double-checked."

The kid's got a theory.

Dak doesn't like it, but he can't dismiss it either.

"Nothing makes sense here, old man." He says logging out

of his computer and pushing his long, athletic frame up from the desk. "All the reports are logged in the database. Filling's waiting on forensics to get back from Wall, but we still haven't gotten the warrant for cell tower data."

"What? How?"

"It's Judge Richards."

Judge Richards, previously a thirty-year defense attorney, had little love for police. Always making sure they dotted every single 'i' with a perfect circle and every 't' crossed with a symmetrical perpendicular line.

"Well fuck. I'll see what I can't do. Judge in today?"

"Beats me, doubt you get ahold of him at this hour anyway. But I'm outta here, Detective Johnson. Have a good one."

Detective Johnson. That's two or three times now.

"Okay, kid. Catch ya tomorrow."

The kid waltzes off without a second remark or anything. *Weird.*

After logging in, Johnson notices the fingerprints have come back. A hit based on some jail time — a possession charge. Nothing crazy, probably wouldn't have even caught cell time today.

But, they've got a picture to go with the name. So, he can run the list of Morgan Humes that they had found and cross-reference with Socials. It does not take long to discover this Morgan Franklin Humes of Fargo, North Dakota, indeed has three *male* friends named Brandon Mitchell, Landon Gaines, and Tristan Caldwell.

Tristan appears quiet on his socials as well. But, Mitchell and Gaines have a *fun* back and forth on Facebook, sharing memories from their annual hiking trip.

"This year we get our boy back! Hitting the Black Hills for the annual bros weekend trip! #NoGirlsAllowed"

Well, this seems like as good of a lead as any.

After an hour and a half of call after call, Dak is at a loss. No one's heard from any of these guys, and their socials are all silent.

The most charismatic of the group, Mitchell, seems to be a real drifter. Relationships, friendships, towns, family; he just moves on to the next one.

Dak runs his fingers along his tailed back dreads, hoping there's something that he's missing. Most of these guys are loners. The kind who peaked in a small town high school, only to realize that in the real world, they weren't jack.

So, we're the only people that want to find you four.

You're all gone well past your return date, and no one reports you missing?

Is that a coincidence or a target?

Coincidence means — right place for the unsubs — wrong place for the bros.

Targeted means the unsub had to know at least one of them, and three of them came from different states.

Only Tristan came from South Dakota. He lived in Rapid City, but the crime scene isn't exactly easy to find. He writes on the whiteboard behind him. *Coincidence.* It has to be that. Targeted would be the situation, not the people.

Alone in the woods. Or near something they shouldn't have been. Maybe Bradley or Tomlinson will have more in the morning.

Dak hasn't seen either since coming in. He wonders if Legends, ever the football captain, sent his team home after a long day.

Still, the question burns through his mind — *Who would be ballsy enough to want to target four grown men in the middle of the woods?*

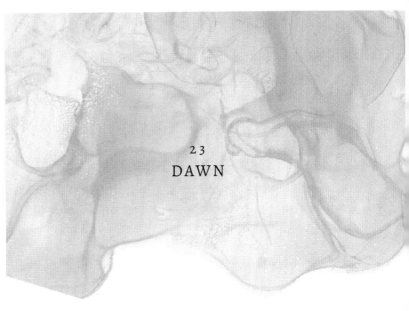

23

DAWN

A t the crack of dawn, most hive members begin to
stir, despite lingering long after the sun has risen.
Not Velvet and Sierra, though.

Today, however, Sierra must go it alone. It's easy for her to
slip out. She zigzags through the woods, ensuring Kari or
someone else isn't following her. When she finally feels safe,
Sierra makes her way to *the mud hole'* as she's been calling it.

Inside, Dezi is there to greet her, "No Velvet?"

"No, she's with the Queen, *remember.*"

"*Right.* How'd she know? I thought it'd be such a mistake to
not prepare any more sisters."

"She's smart our little velvet ant. Speaking of which, where
are they?"

"Exactly where they're supposed to be sis."

"Excellent. And Legends?"

"He's here. Just sat in the corner. Pretty boring guy after
the assimilation."

Sierra's gaze falls on the once vibrant detective, who sits
folded over, neatly crammed into a dark corner of the cave. A

dour expression etched into his once expressive features. "Why's he in his *boxers* Dezi?"

Sierra's hive eyes can pick up the subtle flush of her sister's cheeks. "It's nothing *weird* — I just — I wanted the body heat, ya know, to sleep with." A nervous giggle escapes her sister's throat.

A snort loosens from Sierra as she enjoys the humor all too well. "Noted. Hypnotized versus Assimilated? I take it, there's less personality, and he will still do whatever, and I mean *whatever you want?*" She shoots Dezi a suggestive look, further warming her sister's cheeks.

"I wouldn't know!" The embarrassment cracks Dezi's voice.

Sierra can see Dezi's past. The outcast, the goody-two-shoes, the prude. And she considers what fun it will be to slowly corrupt her sister's sensibilities. Thankfully, without Velvet here, she thinks she might have some time for a spot of fun.

"*Ohhhhh Legends!*" She hollers with a provocative rasp in her voice.

The man silently pivots his vacant gaze up at the pair of them.

"Sierra? What're you doing?"

Sierra lets another snort of laughter blow through her nose.

Isn't it obvious? It's playtime.

Her entire life, the whole world has felt like her plaything. Now, after the assimilation, she has the power to make that a literal reality.

"Legends, boxers off, *now*." With slow trance-like movements, the man draws his boxers over dark and defined thighs, never leaving the damp stone floor. "You can watch if you want." Sierra slides off her boots and yoga pants, revealing herself to the warm morning air.

"Jesus! Sierra! You can't be —"

"If you don't like it, *leave*. But I feel the need for some — *empirical* research. How compliant is he? And of course, I'd be a fool not to investigate what swings between a three-time national champion's legs. Now excuse me, while I get saddled up on that chiseled jaw."

She struts over to the heap of a man. "Legends, *lie down*. Dezi, seriously, if you don't want to be here. Then *don't*. You've got places to be, don't you?"

Dezi's eyes grow wide, revealing all the globular divots of her hive eyes before running off in a panic. Meanwhile, Sierra takes her seat.

I think Velvet will be pleased to know how compliant our detective can be.

"Yeah Samuel, I got it. Yes. I'll get some sleep. Bright and early. Drive safe."

He'd said the *Flandrew* Reservation, but she can't seem to find it on a map. Either she's spelling it wrong, or it's really small. Maybe both?

Samuel'd been cagey with her about the trip initially. Eventually, he'd relented to telling Ghini that even he isn't quite in the know as far as what they're getting into. His 'guy' sounds even dodgier. But Samuel had promised it'd be worth it.

"*If anyone knows anything bout*" — his word had been *monsters* — "*then it's this fella.*"

The only thing left for her to do is call Dak. She owes him a heads up. This time she won't dilly-dally with it. She quickly rings him without a second thought. The ringtone hums while text after text vibrates through simultaneously. She peeks at the screen. It's Todd, her little work puppy.

R u coming to work?

U gud?

One more buzz.

Hmu. Got news!

"Oh, Todd." She whispers to herself out loud.

Dak's voicemail rolls over, and as his deep and gentle voice echoes through Ghini, she gets the sense she won't be seeing her big work pug again. She has no intention of ever going back to the Coke plant. Everything is too real now. How can she expect herself to deal with the normalcy of bottling soda, aching feet, hairnets, and assembly lines?

Beep!

"Oh, shit. Whoops. Sorry Dakota. I uh, yeah, I'm going out of town for a bit. With Samuel. We leave tomorrow morning. Five AM. Headed over to the ass end of the state. Be gone a day or two, but uh, I just wanted to tell you, cuz likely we ain't gonna have much service." She pauses, considering her words carefully. "*Please* — stay safe. I know you're investigating those — *women*, and well, I am too. If this trip goes well, then you'll need to *trust* everything I have to say, cuz — yeah. You're not going to want to believe me. Until then, no need to call me back." She sighs and tacks on, "Thank you my Dakota bear. Thank you for everything."

The room grows eerily silent with the lack of conversation permeating the space. Ghini has nothing to do the rest of the day. She needs something to kill time up until tomorrow morning.

She's not sure she'll sleep tonight. Thankfully, she hasn't taken any Adderall today, the trade-off being that she feels fuzzy without it. Focus seems outside her reach. But, the drug isn't why she worries about sleep.

It's the nerves.

The more she accepts the reality of the situation, the more unnerved she becomes. The anticipation of what's to lay ahead keeps her on her toes like a child the night before Christmas.

She spies the empty bottles of wine strewn across the apartment and decides she knows exactly what to do next.

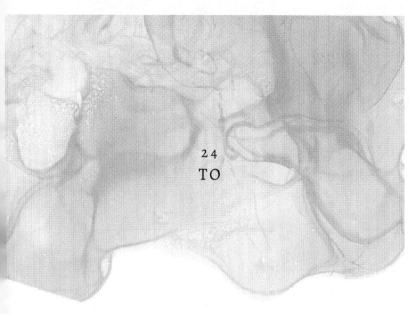

24
TO

"**T**hank you, my dear. Let's grab one of the tents and roll them up in it. Then grab another and roll up their belongings."

How many times has he watched this video, hoping that something, anything, might appear? A flash, a landmark, a bit of audio they'd missed. But there's nothing. As it begins its next loop, Dak hits pause and removes his noise-canceling headphones.

The sounds of the precinct rush back into his prolongedly muffled world. Phones ring, officers chatter with one another, the bright fluorescents hum their little fizzy tunes, and it all echos and reverberates off the linoleum floors and cinderblock walls.

He's spent the last hour watching this footage, and the only thing he's gleaned so far is that the unnamed woman's voice sounds somewhat familiar. Though he's well aware this may be the result of having memorized nearly every millisecond of audio. Yet, clues continue eluding him.

He turns his phone over and the screen flashes a notification for a missed call from Ghini. She's left a voicemail though. She still remembers. He prefers voicemails.

He could use some fresh air and decides to go outside for a cigarette as he listens to the message.

The irony is not lost on him.

The street is quiet and empty as he jaywalks across to the same bench he and Ghini frequent. That last time feels so long ago. He lights his cigarette before pressing play on the recording —

"... *Thank you my Dakota bear. Thank you for everything.*"

Those words. So familiar. A bygone era of his life, but also — there's something else. Something ...

"*Ahh fuck!*"

He's forgotten about the cigarette burning between his fingers, which he just unintentionally used to scar the back of his opposite hand. Looking up he sees Legends strolling toward the precinct.

"Legends! LEGENDS!" Just like the other day, the kid seems to move slower and reacts flatly. But he needs the kid's ears, regardless of how moody he's being. Dak's own are biased, and what's more, there's a similar strangeness to ... to that last time he'd shared this bench with Ghini.

Dak pulls up the photo from the convenience store footage. The woman has a voluptuous head of curls and wears tattered pajamas that we know to have gone missing with Jeannie Freeman. Yet, the woman appears to be the spitting image of his ex-fiance.

Legends lacks his usual saunter when he approaches Dak. "Afternoon, Detective Johnson. You know those things are bad for you." It's the type of thing Legends would playfully chastise him about, yet, any of his usual light-hearted demeanor feels absent.

He syncs the footage up to that end bit where the unknown woman speaks.

"Okay, listen to that one more time." He plays the audio again.

"Thank you, my dear. Let's grab one of the tents . . .

"Now, tell me, does this voice sound *similar* to you?"

" . . . Thank you my Dakota bear. Thank you for everything."

"THAT'S what I'm saying! There wasn't time to explain. I ran for my life! That's the proof you need, isn't it? That they're hunting me. You know they're real, don't you Ghini?"

Velvet watches from the shadows. A flicker of joy bats across her face as she listens in.

"Yes. Yes. Just think of the possibilities. Chat rooms, threads, twits, stories, and all sorts of things that could brainwash and spread mass hysteria — yes. Exactly. That's definitely a possibility. And your poor baby girl —" A long pause fills the room while the trace fragments of the conversation echo across thick stony walls, muffling Dezi's approaching footsteps.

"The girls are all back home. Safe and sound."

Velvet puts a finger to her lips and whispers. "And, how was work?"

"Uneventful. She still ain't showing up, but we got almost everyone now. Haven't heard any suspicions or mention of Stephanie for some time either." Dezi slides the words out with caution.

"No need to fret Dezi. Yes, I decided I could get the ball rolling myself, *since* you decided to never check in." The spurn billows out of her voice and hits Dezi like daggers. "It's okay,

though. I'm still grateful that you brought us Ms. Fumero —
she was a delicious wealth of knowledge."

The volume of the call escalates in an instant. "Wait! Hold
on now. You can't leave town! Don't you want to find your
daughter! — I am calm. You be calm. Listen. — No. *You* listen
to *me*."

Velvet doesn't like where this is going but won't intervene
just yet.

"Yes. Yes. I know. My apologies. I'm a bundle of nerves
lately. Yeah, no, I haven't slept in days. You too, huh . . . Well,
it's nice to know I'm not alone. No. I can't say. But I am in
South Dakota."

A dead silence holds the breath of the cave. Hardly a
whisper departs the earpiece into the soundless void. "Because
we can't. Not yet anyways. It isn't safe. They're looking for me.
— Oh thank you Ghini. But — *shhhhhhhhh!*"

Velvet and Dezi stifle snickers at the dramatic *shushing*.

"Apologies. I thought I'd heard something. There are
others you know? Like us. They know the truth. We just have
to find them and combine our knowledge. Then we get our
loved ones back. There must be a way. At the very least, figure
out every last one of their weaknesses and exploit them."

A loud and quick rattle can be heard from the other end.

"You don't say? Maybe I can tag along. No, no, on second
thought, I don't think it's safe for us to travel together. But I
could meet you there? — Of course. Of course. We don't want
to spook anyone with unwanted visitors."

That nasally chortle blows out her nose, and Velvet notes
how it isn't as skin-crawling to her anymore. "Sorry. I know
it's not funny. But irony like that, can't be ignored. I'll call
again when I have more info and you're back. Maybe then we
can finally meet. Yes. Of course. God speed to you as well."

Sierra closes the phone and sets it on the ground before

springing up toward Dezi and Velvet. "Well, she's going some-where, a *reservation*, to meet with someone who is *supposed* to know more. She didn't say *who* she's going with, but she did seem to confirm your theory — she spoke plenty about her *likkle girl* . . . *Jeannie.*"

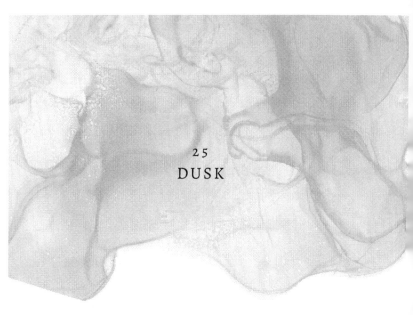

25

DUSK

F ollowing Kari's evening headcount, she isn't surprised that Mel and her lackey are late. Likely out playing daredevil, enjoying the thrill of flirting with death, and intoxicating themselves on the cool night air.

But she also ponders what Queenie told her earlier that afternoon.

An Alpha.

"My dear sweet Kari. You must know something. Our likkle Mel is an Alpha. A rare human capable of becoming a Queen. Think of assimilation like an alpha test. She's essentially already a partial or faux-Queen. Then transitioning to a Complete Queen would be the beta test. But that's a process she can't go through without a special ritual."

Of course, Mel was special. That little bitch.

"But don't let that anger taint you, my sweet daughter. Mel will only ever be compelled to listen to two people. Herself — and me. She has a host of hormones she's trying to understand, and it's best we give her plenty of rope, and if it's too much, she'll hang herself."

That had been the darkest thing she'd ever heard Queenie say. Still, it failed to stifle her envy.

Thankfully, Kari's mother knew just what to say. *"You are my number one. My first daughter. You will always be at my side. Okay?"*

That, Kari understood loud and clear, and something Mel could never take away from her.

As if on cue, with the sun's disappearance beyond the Western ridge, Mel and her sidekick stroll in. That Sierra, with her disgusting snort of a laugh, is just as vile to Kari as the ginger herself. As if sensing her frustration, the dark-haired nuisance goes quiet in an instant. Mel, on the other hand, doesn't so much as bother to flinch.

They continue past her, Mel whispers something snide, but the only word Kari can make out is, *doormat.*

At that, she whips around, incapable of stifling her envious rage. She cries out to her ungrateful sisters, "*Where* have you been? You know Queenie doesn't want to lose any more sisters to exposure. The one was enough." She grabs Mel hard above the elbow, but it's like gripping a steel cable sheathed in leather.

The girl's blue eyes flicker to her bold honeycomb. No one in the colony has anything like them. For a brief second, Kari fears they'll hypnotize her.

Instead, Mel looks to Sierra and says, "Go on. Get some food and go to bed for some sleep." The girl walks off without so much as a peep.

Then her head darts back, and Kari is sure to avoid eye contact. She refuses to be absorbed in those hypnotic pools.

"We don't *risk*. Now you, on the other hand, seem to enjoy risks. Assaulting a sister like this." It's impossible to tell exactly where the girl is looking. Her vibrant cerulean chasms pulsate in such a way that communicates the girl's dissatisfaction regarding Kari's grip on her arm.

"Oh, you want to see assault. I'll show you assault." That anger boils under Kari's chest. Her emotions always feel stronger, as if on instinct, whenever Mel is near.

"*I* don't want that. It seems that *you, want to assault, me.*"

She does. She wants to bash the little bitch's skull in. Ever since Mel hatched, she's been Kari's least favorite sister. She never helps out and is always the first to leave in the mornings. Except for this morning when she had that private talk with Queenie.

"Listen. Queenie would hate to see us like this. Let's get along, don't you think, *Care-Ee?*"

The little buzz-cut twerp has some stones on her.

"She'll understand. Your insolent little ass needs whooped. Fuck getting along. I know you're up to something out there. I don't know what, but I'm-a put a fucking stop to it." She's tried to follow the brat and her clique on several occasions, but her need to be near Queenie, and help with the newborns, was a compulsion Kari couldn't ignore.

"So much crass language, sister. It's sad to see you behave this way. To think I looked up to you. Clearly, you're not the sister who looks out for her siblings. Probably grew up an only child. *Spoiled*. That'd be my guess."

The girl's smirk rockets up the side of her face briefly, before she attempts to walk off. But Kari maintains a vice grip on Mel's arm. She doesn't think twice before lifting the ginger bitch off the ground — she's hardly a paperweight to Kari — and hurls her against the cave wall. The immense collision sends a shudder through the tunnels causing earth to sprinkle down on them from above.

"Listen here you little cunt."

"*Woah.* That's no way to talk to your sister?" Her blue

honeycombs pulsate a tantalizing rhythm, but Kari refuses to focus on them.

"Oh you're lucky that's all I called you."

"Well, I wouldn't say lucky. You did call me a bitch too. Not to mention, threw me twenty feet through the air into a wall of stone. Seems pretty aggey to me."

"I'll show you fuckin' aggey." Kari loves the endorphin rush of sprinting. She feels light as a feather, bounding the distance between them in three steps. More debris falls from above as she slams into Mel at full speed.

"*ENOUGH!*" Queenie's voice shakes the entirety of the cave system.

It's not just Queenie. Sierra and the entire colony stand behind her. As many as thirty women. A sea of multicolored honeycombs all lock on Kari. None worse than Queenie's golden-amber wells, which pull Kari from her body.

The next thing she knows, Mel and Queenie are standing behind her. Kari feels rooted to where she stands. Her forearm locked in its outstretched position to where she'd pinned Mel to the wall. Embarrassment screams *run*, but she can't.

"Everything will be okay my *likkle scarlet joy.*"

Queenie's presence is larger than life, and Kari wants nothing more than to shrink away and hide. She feels smaller than ever next to her. Her mother's presence makes Kari want to revert to her childhood. To be that little girl who'd fit into the space under the bed, where she could hide and no one would be able to reach her.

"Kari. We talked earlier."

"Yes." Tears already stream down her face. *What have I done?*

"I had no idea that you were capable of such anger. Is the euphoria of the sisterhood not enough for you to live a happy life?"

"It is." She says as tears continue coating her cheeks. Snot thickens in her nose. The trauma of childhood asthma wreaks havoc on her mind. She feels like a pathetic little girl. The sort of pathetic that comes with memories of beatings clawing their way from her cloudy memories.

"What are you doing?"

Kari hasn't moved. She can't understand what the question means.

"Kari, your vibrations. Do you think I am going to strike you? Like you struck poor Mel?"

She meekly nods her reply, taking note that at some point, she had flinched into a meek defensive position.

"Oh, my sweet child. *Relax.*" Queenie helps lower her arm before bringing Kari in for a hug — thawing her frozen body.

Thank you. This is why you are my Queenie. My mother. I will do anything for you.

"THANK YOU, my Queenie. I am sorry you had to raise your voice and intervene. I feel awful." It is true. Queenie can tell.

"Oh my likkle Mel, there's no need for your apologies. At our core," she grabs at her chest, "we are women, and when a bunch of strong women are confined to one place, fighting is almost pre-ordained."

She sounds so wise. Different from the first day they'd met.

"I am so impressed by you, my mother."

"And I, you, daughter." She smiles, showing off her big white teeth framed by a jaw resembling the stark angles of a diamond.

"Queenie, most sisters have been calling me Velvet, and it's okay if you want to too."

"Oh, child. You were Mel when you were born, and you will always be Mel to me." She hugs her in tight, and whispers into her daughter's ear, "Now tell me, why were you late?" The question has the intended effect of catching her off guard. She feels Mel tense ever so slightly in her arms.

"I should know better, it's just." The girl pauses and Queenie feels the rehearsal of it, the lack of genuineness ebbs from her daughter. "I'm super strong now. I have these amazing reflexes. I'm not the shy pudgy outcast that gets made fun of for being a ginger anymore. I'm finally able to go out into the world and be confident. I know I'm supposed to be more mature, but at heart, I want that life, ya know? To have fun without caring about being judged."

Queenie kisses Mel atop her fuzzy head. "You are sweet. I can understand that. But, we have responsibilities. You are a big sister to many. See how they look up to you?"

"*To me?* They look up to *me?*"

"Yes. Remember that and act accordingly. Now, tomorrow morning, you will join me to discuss your idea one last time. But for now, *go to sleep* — I mean, *bed. Go to bed.*"

"Of course mother, anything you say." The girl gazes up and around, her eyes flicker, and she saunters off without a word.

You have the rope little scarlet one, do not disappoint me.

ACKNOWLEDGMENTS

Thank you to everyone in the Kindle Vella community where *Season of The Monster* was exclusively serialized.

There were so many fantastic individuals who helped me grow as a writer, a marketer, and even as a reader. This is a passionate and devoted community of writers, to which, I am wholeheartedly grateful.

Specifically, I want to throw thanks to Azrielle Lawless for giving me my first ever interview. I had so much fun, and you opened doors for me to keep moving.

Tess Combs, you literally financed my first-ever ad campaign. No, it wasn't much, but you saw something that made you believe in me and SOTM. For that, I am indebted to you.

Zack Lester, man you rock, and you know it. I'm glad I've got a guy in this world that I can turn to about all this writing stuff. It also helps that you're as mad a hatter as I!

Tirzah Hawkins, I could devote pages to you here. Your advice, your support, your inspirational success, the works you've put out there to help educate new authors like me, your lack of gate-keeping — I mean seriously, I could go on forever. You're an amazing human, and I value you so much.

Then there's Meg Fitz and Gage Greenwood. Meg, you asked all the questions so that people like me could follow in your footsteps, thank you! Gage, you answered a lot of those questions. Not only that, but you inspire me with your kindness, your support, and your tenacity in many facets of life. Thank you!

Of course, I don't know where I would be without my Story Stash peeps like Jen Sequel, Des Sweets, Coda Languez, C.L. Slias, Kell Frillman, Kim Riehle, Liz Johnson, LJ Vitanza, Tasha Creed, S RC Johnson, and those other members I've already mentioned. You all are extended family at this point!

Lastly, and **most importantly**, I must acknowledge someone who probably doesn't want me to do so . . . but if it weren't for her, I wouldn't be here today. So, to save her anonymity, I will say . . .

To the woman, I once called, my *Pumpkin Spiced Iced Latte*,

Thank you.

We had sat down one day at the University of Illinois - Urbana-Champaign with our dogs, and I had told you that I wanted to write a new monster mythology. I told you my ideas, and you helped me whittle them down until we both settled on the idea of wasps. Thanks to you, we ironed out what that would look like.

Not only that, but you believed in me when most people didn't. You supported me when most people wouldn't. If it weren't for you, *Season of The Monster* would never have existed.

I am beyond grateful to you for all that you did for me.

I'm sorry it turned out that I was the one who had a monster inside them. I'm working on it though. I'm giving that thing something to fear.

I hope you and the *'likklest one'* are happy and healthy.

SNEAK PEAK OF PART II

SUMMER

TURN THE PAGE FOR A FIRST LOOK

Season of The
Monster [S2] :...
AJ Humphreys

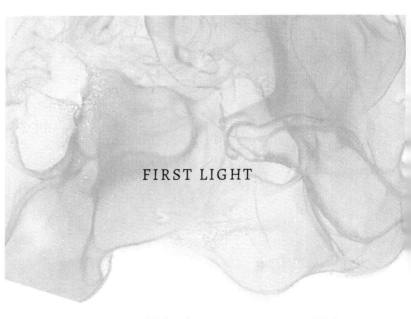

FIRST LIGHT

Todd is grateful for this warm morning air. He knows summer heat and humidity are right around the corner, but ever since he and Maria began dating, life has been, well, *magical*. This morning is one of the most yet.

The sun has barely poked its first rays over the eastern Badlands. The sky glows with a bounty of colors as he and Maria enjoy their morning stroll alongside her little Yorkie, Kelso. He's a goofball of a dog, but Todd is as much infatuated with Kelso as he is Maria.

This morning they're walking around the House of Japan Gardens. A quaint little area with cherry-blossom trees, a veiny spiderweb of footpaths, and four miniature ponds that geese love to frequent. Each separated by old-fashioned arcing red Japanese garden bridges and grass mounds perfect for a picnic — when not covered in goose shit.

They take a fork on one of the paths and Kelso goes to sniff the bush in the center of the intersecting stony walkways. Maria gives him a quick tug, pulling him up by his harness, and calls for a 'heel.' Only, the little goober won't give up his desperate attempts at getting his sniffer into that bush. Thankfully, it seems that a training treat from Maria's fanny-pack is motivation enough to bring him back to her side — however, not without engaging in one last stare down against that pesky bush.

Todd looks back wondering what the little guy smells. Maybe some birds or squirrels have taken up refuge in there. Though it's more likely some lazy asshole just shoved their garbage between the branches. Or another dog marked it, or —

Wait what was that?

"Did you hear that?" Maria had heard it too.

It sounds silly to Todd, but he could have sworn he heard — *giggling*.

"I don't know. Maybe?" He looks down into her big caramel eyes. "It kinda sounded like . . ." He looks back to the bush as the path bends around one of the ponds. "Ah, never mind. I think it's just a bit early and we're hearing things."

"Oh, my big baby. Are you spooked handsome?" Maria laughs and playfully nudges him with her arm.

He knows they have to be a funny sight. She's all of 5'1" in her running shoes, while Todd stands nearly seven feet tall. But she's been good for him. It hasn't been a long *official* relationship, but it's been the best he's ever had. Their ritual involves walking Kelso early in the mornings, which has been helping his knees and hips more throughout the day. They still ache, but nowhere near as bad.

"As long as I have you, I can never be spooked, my beautiful Latin goddess." He leans down and offers his lady a kiss, which she takes with a fervor that lets him know what's in store when they get back to her house.

"Where have you been all my life Todd Powell?"

"Right here. I'm kinda hard to miss!" It's one of those moments of laughing together, where everything seems to be in sync throughout the world.

Now hand in hand, they follow Kelso's lead as he tugs against his harness to take the bridge over one of the ponds. It's a bit darker on here, as a large grove of trees blots out a patchwork of the morning's rays.

A fluttering sound catches Todd's attention. It looks like Kelso may have heard it too because they both turn and look around them. All Todd sees are the groves of cherry blossoms.

Suddenly, Maria cries out. A piercing screech slices through the early morning air. Her legs come out from under her, yet Todd somehow manages to catch her by the armpit before she wipes out entirely. Right as he seizes her mid-descent, Todd notices the sheer terror carved into her face.

"What happened?"

"I slipped on something." She huffs out through ragged breaths.

Todd looks around and can sort of make out something on the bridge. It's a pile, but the shadows and early morning colors make it hard to discern anything beyond an amorphous blob. Todd's first thought is goose shit, but still feels enough sense of curiosity to pull his phone out and flip on the flashlight.

Instantly, Maria gasps loud enough that a group of robbins decide to flutter off at the minor disturbance. She rips Kelso back to her side, keeping him close. "Dios Mio! Is that what I think it is, Todd?"

Todd crouches his giant frame down to get a closer look. His knees pop like a firecracker going off. What he finds as he settles on his heels, is a pile of — *meat*. Red meat. It looks too lean to be from the usual suspects, but maybe someone dropped their groceries, and its shape has just changed from sitting out overnight.

He can see where Maria's heal caught the edge of the pile and she slid forward. It had to have been close to a foot in length, so no wonder she was startled.

"Todd, I don't like this. I think I just heard someone — *giggling*."

Todd nearly leaps out of his crouch, back to his feet at that word — *giggling*. With a cautious strength, he rests his hand on the small of her back. He wants her to know he's here for her.

"Listen, if you're out there, this ain't funny!" He looks back to Maria and takes her hand in his. "Let's get movin', we got a long day ahead, anyway."

She smiles at him. Maria is strong and does well to hide her fear, but Todd can see the panic pressing against her soft round features. He'll be the strong one. Getting them back home without issue is his main priority right now. He knows it's all probably nothing, but quickly takes a photo of the meat pile, feeling that if it isn't *nothing*, and it is *something*, he'll need to prove it to someone.

As he steps off the bridge, he knows he's heard that giggling again. Maria must have heard it too because she looks up to him. Deep, doe-like wide eyes express worry and fear. He keeps a tight hold on her hand, and she returns the favor. He can't help but find an appreciation for how strong the tiny woman's grip is.

Suddenly, there's that fluttering sound again. It's subtle and quiet, but unmistakable. They increase their pace and Todd does his best to not let his strides get too long. But Maria's no slouch and hurries her legs with a fervor that only shorter women can accomplish.

WOOOF WOOOF WOOOF!

Kelso's barks shatter the heart-pounding silence before

quickly turning to a guttural growl. The sun peaks over the hills, showering the little pathway in a sea of warm golden glow. Just then, two women appear. The pair appear over-dressed, wearing thermals, vests, and stocking caps on this warm summer morning.

Kelso continues to bark and growl. His ears pin straight back against his skull. Maria holds his leash tightly, fighting off the dog's continued lurches and yaps.

One of them, a young, dark-skinned girl steps forward, "Good morning. How's it going?" She has an unsettling sneer on her face.

Todd places himself between the girls and Maria, who has managed to wrangle Kelso to her side. Todd is not sure what *this* is, but the situation feels wrong. Like one false move could mean life or death. It's a sense he's honed throughout his life-time. "We just walking. What you and yours doing?"

Maria screams before Todd realizes anything has happened. Slowly, his mind registers a tight burning pinch in his thigh. Eating away at his nerves as if he'd just poured rubbing alcohol or *IcyHot* all over a series of deep cuts. That's when he looks down, finally noticing that the other girl is right there in front of him.

In his space.

Dark curly black hair hangs just above her shoulders. She looks familiar, but he can't place from where he'd know a little white girl.

"Hi there. I'm Sierra. And, you and I, we're gonna be friends."

Todd looks down past the girl's unsettling grin to see her pale fingers end at his shorts. No, not end. Her fingernails are completely buried into the meat of his thigh. There's an unset-tling fluid pumping beneath the surface of her fingers. It's like something out of a nightmare. Whatever the liquid is, looks to be flowing toward the fingernails concealed within his quad. He can feel it pulsing and burning as it enters his bloodstream, like a hot injection.

This can't be real!

The last things he sees before blacking out, are Kelso hightailing it out of the park with the leash flapping behind him, and the other girl — the little sister with the sneer on her face — standing over Maria.

He only thinks about what could've been. This woman whom he'd thought was helping him find happiness. A life he could tell his best friend, Ghini, about. Maybe then one day their kids could all have play dates, while Jeannie babysat…

Instead, there is the reality of the moment. Maria is fighting to stay knelt, clutching at her throat. A deep, dark scarlet courses between her fingers, while a gurgling cough worms its way across her lips. The sister's hand is held high. As if in slow motion Todd notes her fingertips, capped with tiny barbs, drip that same visceral red.

It appears to glow as each drop falls to the Earth below, reflecting a similar color from the sky behind's first dawning lights.

ABOUT THE AUTHOR

AJ Humphreys is an emerging author of thrillers, horrors, and mysteries. Season of The Monster | SPRING is his debut novel.

When AJ isn't writing he can often be found in a hammock reading, maybe while camping, but almost always with his best buddy, Kobe The Husky at his side. Together, they both enjoy hiking and swimming, especially.

He also operates as an amateur landscape and wildlife photographer, which fits in well with his thirst for outdoor adventuring.

Subscribe to *The Authors' Journey* Newsletter at readajhvellas.com and stay in the loop on new releases, serial writings, as well as merchandise, photography, and other fun giveaways/announcements.

AJ currently lives in Urbana, IL, and writes full-time.

AJ loves to connect with readers and writers, so make sure to check out all of his social media platforms!

a amazon.com/kindle-dbs/entity/author/B0B51ZHPXJ
f facebook.com/ajhumphreyswrites
g goodreads.com/ajhumphreys
o instagram.com/ajhumphreyswrites
♪ tiktok.com/@aj_humphreys
🐦 twitter.com/ajhumphreys2

Made in the USA
Middletown, DE
09 September 2024

60089721R00091